D1524078

THE VAMPIRE'S SLAVE

By Zara Novak

By Zara Novak

CHAPTER ONE

Claire

CLAIRE WALKED INTO HER APARTMENT, shut the door behind her, and threw her keys to the side with an exasperated sigh.

It had been a long day. After working nine hours in the hospital, she also had to make an impromptu appearance at her older sister's baby shower. Claire had enjoyed herself, but the screaming women and the jealousy inside of her had proved too much to handle. Lisa was only a little older, and she already had everything. It didn't help that Lisa had arranged the shower on the same day as Claire's eighteenth birthday, but she didn't care. Her family always forgot about her. She was used to it.

That wasn't the real reason she'd left the party early. She'd wanted a baby more than anything for the longest time. Celebrating her sister's *amazing* womb was only a painful reminder that Claire was single and very much not pregnant.

She stopped and stared at herself in the hallway mirror, twisting the small cross around her neck between her fingers.

"Bring me a man, Lord," she whispered into the mirror. "And bring me babies too. Lots of them."

Taking a deep breath, she held the prayer in her head for a moment before dropping the ornament back to her chest. It was no use anyway. She'd made a thousand prayers just like that one, and none of them ever came to fruition. She felt with her fuller figure she wasn't attractive to men, not the ones she was interested in anyway. If God wouldn't answer her call, maybe it was time for her to find something else to worship.

Tired of looking at the sorry girl in the mirror, she kicked her shoes off and started down the hallway when a knock came from the door.

Odd.

Claire looked down at her wristwatch and saw it was close to 10 p.m.—a little late for guests, and she wasn't expecting company.

She walked back to the door and squinted through the peephole, only to see the fish eye image of the empty hallway.

Confused, she opened the door to see a beautiful man with ice-white skin standing in the space that had been empty just a second earlier. Claire swallowed at something in her throat, feeling flushed.

"Good evening. Can I help you?"

She looked at the stranger, almost hypnotized by his beauty. His outfit was smart. It looked expensive, it was tailored, and it favored his athletic body extremely well. Dark jeans, neat dress shoes, and a dark sweater clung to the attractive curves of his muscular torso. He was handsome, with a chiseled face and a strong jaw. His hair was dark and thick, and groomed to look tussled. Every part of him screamed perfection.

"Eric Belmont. I just moved in across the hall and thought I'd introduce myself." He smiled at her, his peculiar blood-red eyes twinkling like dark rubies.

Eric held his hand in Claire's direction. She shook it, feeling intimidated by his beauty.

"Eric... I'm Claire. Claire Eldridge. It's lovely to meet you."

Their hands parted and Claire's eyes flicked to his hand. No ring.

She wanted to turn to the mirror and whisper a "Thank you, God." Was he the answer to her prayers?

Her elation faded fast. Eric would never fall for a girl like her. Between his designer stubble and perfectly sculpted hair, it was most obvious he took care of himself. He probably enjoyed the company of only the most beautiful women, and Claire did not consider herself to be a beautiful woman. She enjoyed her chocolate, and she had the curves to show for it. Eric probably had a phone book full of stick-thin supermodels at his disposal.

"Well?" Eric stood in expectation outside her apartment.

"...Well?" Claire repeated his words, unsure of his meaning.

"Aren't you going to invite me inside?"

For a strange man knocking on her door at such a late hour, alarm bells should have been going off in Claire's head, but they didn't. His sheer beauty was too distracting. She tripped over herself apologizing, bumbling for him to come in.

"O-Of course, Eric! Sorry!" She stepped to one side, and a chill passed through her body as the stranger moved through the doorway.

Claire stopped for a second to ask herself *why* she was allowing a stranger into her home, but pushed the thought to the back of her mind. Being friendly with neighbors had never been high on her priority list. If the rest of them looked liked this, she *might* reconsider.

She closed the door and noticed how Eric's feet had barely seemed to move when he walked in, almost as if he were sliding over ice. She took a deep breath to relax herself.

All right, Claire. Time to play hostess.

"You must forgive me Eric, I—"

He had barely walked into the apartment before spinning on his heels and sliding back down the hallway to crush Claire against the front door. His right arm was parallel with the floor, wedged between her chest and her throat. His other hand clutched her coat, pinning her up against the door. She opened her mouth to scream, but his hand clasped over it, silencing her completely.

"You will be very quiet. And you will stay quiet. Is that clear?"

Claire nodded and he removed his hand from her mouth, lowering her back down to the floor. Her heart spun in her chest, swirling with adrenaline and fear, but there was something else inside her, something that was almost shameful: abject carnal arousal.

His sparkling red eyes flicked up and down, taking her body in. Claire stood with her chest heaving, wringing her hands with angst. Terror pricked through her body. What was his motive? What was his intention?

He stared at a spot on her chest and snarled before reaching his hand out and clutching at her cross. He tore the ornament from around her neck, breaking the chain as he did so.

Eric turned and launched the cross somewhere into the apartment behind him, only to look back at Claire a second later. He stared at her like a flesh-starved lion.

"W–What are you going to do with me?"

Eric laughed. "My dear Claire. The better question is what am I *not* going to do with you?"

Claire backed against the door.

"You're crazy! Don't kill me! Please!"

The deep rumbling laugh came from his chest once more and his blood-red eyes rose to hers. A dark smile etched across his face.

"My dear Claire, why on earth would I *kill you*? I'd do nothing so wasteful. Oh no."

"But I don't understand! What do you want from me then?!" Reaching behind her back, she secretly tried to grasp the door handle.

"I will not hurt you, darling. I will mate you."

"Mate me?!"

"Why yes. I want to put a baby inside you."

*

Before Claire could respond he was on her, dragging her through the apartment, pulling her into the kitchen. Only then did Claire find the strength within her to try to stop him. Beautiful or not, she couldn't just let this man barge his way into her home and assault her.

"Stop, stop this!"

His grasp loosened and she wriggled free, realizing that he'd *let* her escape. There had only been a brief display of his strength so far—he had held her against the door as if she weighed nothing, but it was enough to assert that he could overpower her whenever he wanted.

Breath racing, she stared at the man in bewilderment. She knew she should try to escape, but there was something holding her back. She didn't want him to leave. Her last few years had been lonely. Thirsting for attention, she acted out of desperation. He was dangerous, but his beauty was so hypnotic. There was shame inside of her for craving his attention, even if it threatened her life.

Part of her wanted to reason with him; part of her wanted to believe the beautiful man standing in her apartment wasn't that bad. In a shameful sense, she knew the reality of her motive. If he left, she might never see him again, and that was the most terrifying prospect of all.

"What are you saying?! I'm not going to just let you put a baby in me!"

"Oh you will. Don't worry. In time you will beg me for it."

Eric smiled, baring his teeth. Claire stared in horror as his teeth grew from his mouth like ivory knives. She backed away, shaking her head.

"Y-You're a..."

"...vampire." He finished the sentence for her, winking as he did so. Her last shred of hope dissipated—there was nothing here to salvage. This man was no man at all; he was a demon, a dark servant of the black prince.

"Get out! Get out!" Claire backed away, shrieking at Eric. She had invited him in, and she shouldn't have done that. But he had to leave if she asked him. Right?

Eric walked toward her, laughing. He found amusement in her terror at first, but he grew tired of it fast. The times for games had passed, and his impatience was growing thin.

"Silence."

Claire backed into a cabinet and fell quiet, her whole body falling in stillness.

"You invited me in...yes, but I'm *in* now. That's it. There's no kicking me out. Do not worry. I will cause you no harm. If I intended to hurt you, you would be dead by now."

Eric pulled a long silver knife from his jacket.

"See?" He placed the knife back into his jacket, like he wasn't interested in it at all.

"I'd never hurt you. I would be a mad man to slit your throat—I'm sure your blood is... *delicious.*" Eric's ruby-red eyes grazed over her body once more like she was a prize steak. "But you have something much more valuable. I've been watching you for some time now Claire, waiting for you to reach your Red Moon."

"R-Red Moon?"

"Your eighteenth birthday. I first found you some time ago, and I've been following you since then, waiting for you to ripen."

"B-But why me? Pick one of the other million girls that would have you!"

Eric smirked, and Claire sensed he'd interpreted her comment as a compliment.

"Most people can't breed with vampires. ...It's not that we're not able." He glanced down at his crotch as if he knew something. "But it's an intense process that kills most on the receiving end."

Claire swallowed.

"But you—Claire—*you* are one of the rare few. Hyper-fertile, genetically predisposed to be a breeder."

"A *breeder?*"

"Yes," Eric said beneath a knowing smile. "One who can stand the raw intensity of the vampire..."

The thought intoxicated her. In some respects, he offered something she'd always wanted. But she never expected it to happen like this. For a servant of the devil, he *was* awfully tempting.

Out of the corner of her eye she saw the small cross on the floor, which Eric had torn from her throat just minutes ago.

"No." Claire steeled her jaw. "I won't be some fertile servant for an agent of darkness."

He laughed, long and hard.

"Please, Claire. Let's not be so rude. Turn down the amateur dramatics. What's wrong with me? Don't you find me attractive?"

"Well..." Claire's eyes darted around the kitchen, trying not to meet his, her cheeks flushing with red.

"Am I not?" Eric stepped close, pushing his body against hers.

Warm tingles surged across her body at his touch.

"You're handsome. So what? That's not just cause for you to burst in here, threaten me, and tell me you want to impregnate me!"

"Oh Claire. Claire, Claire, Claire. You're such a divine beauty. Why can't you understand?"

"What are you talking about?! Understand what?"

"I'm afraid you haven't got a *choice,* my most beautiful darling."

"What?!"

"You *want* me. Are you so naïve you can't *see* that? You *want* me, Claire. You *want* me and you *want* me *bad.*"

"No..." Claire shook her head, trying to deny his accusations. "You're full of yourself, you're clueless, men... you're all the same!"

He smiled this time, repeating his words once more in a low whisper. Time slowed to a crawl.

"You *want* me."

His voice compelled her, coursing through every inch of her flesh, spinning through her veins like dark roots, twining around her soul itself. She repeated the words back to him.

"...I *want* you?"

Her speech was slow and tired. Everything was getting hazy.

"Yes," Eric said. "Don't you know?"

He rolled his neck on his shoulders and then his eyes were on her again in an instant, but they were different now, glimmering with intensity like pearls of twinkling blood.

"Strip."

"Strip?"

"*Strip.*"

Before she realized what she was doing, Claire's hands pulled her clothes from her body, betraying her mind and her own intentions.

However Eric was doing this, he seemed to have direct control over her, like his word had complete power over her mind and body. As his effect infected her treacherous hands, it infected her mind too, and within a few seconds of his utterance, Claire didn't feel compelled to follow his orders—she *wanted* to follow them.

He was so beautiful, so mysterious, but apprehension held her back. She wanted this, no matter how much he wanted to convince her.

She dropped her coat to the floor, pulled her spaghetti strap tank top over her head, and unclasped her bra, revealing her large milky white breasts.

Next she unzipped her pencil skirt, removed her tights, and stepped out of her white cotton panties. She stood before him nude now, waiting in nervous expectation.

She wasn't sure why she had followed his instructions so blindly, but at the same time, she wasn't sure why she'd ever wanted to ignore it.

"Good girl." Eric's eyes sparkled with want as he looked the young girl up and down. "Now, bend over, I want to see that delicious pussy of yours."

Claire steeled herself again. Clarity swept over her for a brief second, and she realized this was too much, it was too fast.

"N-No..." Her mouth protested, but once again her body was turning, betraying her as his intention washed over her.

Her feet turned until she stood facing the counter. She bent over, placing her weight on her elbows. She inched her feet apart, giving him the best glimpse possible.

"No!" Her voice came back to her. "I don't want your dark babies inside of me!"

"Oh, Claire." She heard Eric laughing as he approached from behind her. "You talk so *funny*. All that will come with good time. This is just to get you ready."

"Ready?"

"I want to *taste* you. I should wait, I really should. But your scent is so delicious. I don't think I can wait any longer. Just a little taste, it's ...it's all I want."

His power swelled over her once more, silencing her mind and thoughts. Hands, cold as winter ice, slid up the back of her thighs, coursing upward, smoothing across her soft and naked skin.

Claire's heart raced underneath her as she reacted to his touch, warmth swelling inside of her at his hypnotic power.

He wrapped his fingers around the front of her thighs, stroking down from the crease of her hip, stopping just above her knees.

More than anything, Claire wanted him to touch her *there*. The space between her legs throbbed with want for his cold and silken touch.

"Please..." she whimpered, surprised to find that her mouth was now working. "Please touch me."

And he did.

She gasped in delight as his tongue pushed against her dripping cunt, sliding up, tasting her juices.

"F-Fuck!" She squeaked the words out in a half gasp, overwhelmed by the sensation of him licking her pussy. She sunk her teeth into her lower lip, clenched her fists, and hummed in pleasure as his thumbs squeezed into the back of her thighs.

He lapped at her over and over again, soft, fast, long and slow, always changing pace, always keeping her guessing, always building her pleasure.

Her body rocked and tensed in response, trying to contain the pleasure as it threatened to spark across her. He moved his hands up the inside of her thighs, pulling her apart gently, only to push his tongue inside of her, probing the inner edge of her canal.

"Yes, yes!" Claire balled her fist, slamming it down onto the marble countertop. Her thighs trembled as her orgasm threatened to burst.

Eric whispered from behind her, taking a second to let his lips part from hers. "You are so delicious."

Claire gasped as his finger slipped inside of her, gliding upward into her body until he had reached his knuckle. With his other hand he slipped his finger up between her legs, massaging the button at her front, while lapping at her folds.

She tried to focus her attention on all of his affection, as it was all intoxicating, but it was too much to contain. Breath shaking, she dropped her head to the counter, pushing her ass back as he brought her to her climax.

"Eric, yes... Eric!" She wasn't afraid to say his name anymore, she wasn't afraid to enjoy his affection. The pad of his middle finger pushed hard against her clit, massaging her juices in small hard circles. The tip of his tongue grazed her up and down, sending shivers through her spine. The finger inside of her brushed up and down her walls, pulsing warmth across her core.

"Yes!"

She came hard, balling her fists and eyes so tight her whole body trembled.

His fingers squeezed into the supple flesh of her hips, pulling her pussy against his mouth as she came, lapping greedily as her cream pulsed onto his tongue. He lapped her up, taking it all in, savoring the sweet and delicate tastes of her juices.

The warmth crested, and sprang across her body once more, rocking her hips, shaking her thighs, melting the rest of the world away, until she could take no more.

When Claire came to, she was on her back on the kitchen floor, legs spread, hands up on either side of her face, completely naked. Eric sat on the floor just across from her, clothed, staring at her with a wicked smile.

Claire sat up, brushing her hair from her face, too lust-drunk to care he had gotten his way with her. If his mouth was that good, would the other parts be even better?

"You'll come to know soon enough." Eric laughed.

"What?"

"The rest of me works just as well, if not better," he said. Standing, he helped Claire up too.

"You can read my thoughts?"

"There's a lot I can do, dear sweet Claire. All this you'll come to know soon, back at my castle."

"Castle?"

"Why yes." Eric's eyes darted around Claire's apartment. "You wouldn't expect me to consummate your womb here do you? It's best for the heir if we're on hallowed soil."

Eric took Claire's hand into his own, but she pulled away, shaking her head. He might have had a hold on her before, but she took back control briefly. Everything about this was wrong. She didn't want this. Eric might be beautiful, but he was dangerous.

"You can't take me from here. This is my home. This is where I live."

"Not anymore," he laughed again. "You're coming with me. Whether you like it or not."

He rushed toward her and before Claire could scream, he had thrown her over his shoulder and was moving through her apartment, away from the front door.

"Where are we going?!" Claire kicked and hammered at Eric as she watched the floor of her apartment rush below her. "The door is that way!"

"We're not using the door. We're heading out the back."

Claire heard the patio slide open, and shivered as a gust of wind swept in from outside, chilling her naked rear.

"But we're on the third floor! And what about my clothes?!"

"You don't deserve clothes," Eric said as he climbed onto the balcony railing. "If you want clothes, you must act like a good slave."

Eric swung Claire over his shoulder, holding her in his arms. She clung tightly as he crouched down on the rail, poised like a cat. She glanced down at the street below, body shivering in the cold of the night. They were so high. Just one wrong step, and they'd be dead.

A cruel and ghastly roar bellowed from Eric's throat, startling Claire. She looked at him in abject terror as two dark wings burst from his back, shearing the clothes from his torso. The wings spread themselves, stretching across Claire's small balcony, and that of her neighbors' too. He stood up again, stretching, breathing a sigh of relief.

"Let's fly."

The ground rushed toward them and Claire tightened her grip on Eric, closing her eyes. He flexed his wings, filling them with two giant pockets of air. Then they swept upward, soaring up and into the cold of the dark night.

CHAPTER TWO

Eric

BY THE TIME THEY TOUCHED DOWN AT THE CASTLE, Claire was nearly frozen solid. Eric scorned himself for being so careless with the girl. When they had left, he thought that carrying her naked through the air would have been a fun punishment for her, but as soon as he saw her blue lips he knew it was a mistake.

He had been infatuated from the moment he had first seen her and smelled her scent on the subway all those months ago. And to think, she had only been a short time away from her Red Moon. He was in the city on business for the family, and as luck would have it, he'd happened to stumble across Claire.

As soon as he caught her scent it had dominated his every waking minute. He hadn't wanted to let the girl out of his sight, but even when he had to, he'd still been able to feel a slight signal from her. When he bonded with her, he'd always have a faint sense of where she was in the world, no matter how far—not that it mattered. Eric didn't have any intentions of letting her leave his sight from this point onward.

As he filled the tub with hot water and fragrant soap, Claire sat shaking until the steaming water swelled around her, bringing heat back to her bones once more.

"I apologize for that." Eric said, turning off the bronze tap once the tub was full. The color had returned to Claire's cheeks now and she was looking a lot happier. "I forget how fragile humans can be. Cold isn't something that I've had to think about for hundreds of years."

Claire's eyes widened at his admission. Eric held his breath and waited for the question that he had heard a thousand times before, but it didn't come.

"Your house. This castle...it's beautiful, Eric.

Eric opened and closed his mouth several times, somewhat stunned. He hadn't expected that. Girls always wanted to know how old he was. It always made him feel like a spectacle. It always reminded him that he wasn't human—he was in fact vampire. It was the sweet curse that haunted his every waking moment.

"You don't... you don't want to know how old I am?"

Claire sank lower into the tub, until the steaming water was at her delicious throat. "I've seen enough vampire films to know that you're probably eight hundred or something." Claire laughed. "I don't really care. You look phenomenal; it doesn't matter how old you are, I guess."

Eric smiled and almost felt warmth within him at her comment.

"You have a nice home, Eric," Claire said, looking around the marble bathroom.

"Thank you. Castle Belmont has been in our family for many generations. We've spent quite a lot of time seeing that the space we live in is well looked after."

He looked around the bathroom himself. Thick slabs of black and white marble, golden sconces, black chandeliers. It was all decidedly Gothic, with a modern flourish. There was a deliberate darkness about the castle. Any light source was usually candles. If it had to be artificial, then older bulbs were preferable. There was something about the cold incandescent LED bulbs that just didn't sit right with Eric or the inhabitants of Belmont. The same could be said for most things. The modern world just didn't seem to agree with undead blood. His oldest sister, Veronica, had been insistent that they all get smartphones when they first came out, but the devices had all fried themselves within a week.

"We?"

"What, you didn't just think I lived here all by myself, did you? My family is in the castle too. Albeit far away. Most of this floor is mine. You can expect privacy."

They were in a bathroom on the ninth floor in the northeast corner of the castle, the corner which sat directly on the cliff tops, perched over the mountains below. There was a small diamond-crossed window on the north wall of the bathroom, adjacent to the head of the bath. Eric had Ira see to it that all the windows in the castle had been UV coated. The light still wasn't pleasant for him, but it made walking around in the day tolerable at least.

He turned his attention back on Claire, grazing his eyes over her naked body. Her large breasts bobbed in the water as she lay in the bronze-footed tub, savoring the warmth. Claire opened her eyes and saw that Eric was staring at her.

"Sorry." Eric didn't know why he was apologizing. Especially to a human. She was his slave and he could do with her as he wished.

There was a small part of him, however, that sensed there was something different about this girl. It was a rare enough thing to find a breeder—the rare hyper-fertile humans that could withstand the force of a vampire in full heat. It was another thing for him to see a woman so beautiful, and another thing completely for her to be nude before him in the bath.

He had grown sick and tired of the endless harem of stick-thin girls that had thrown themselves at him in years gone by. His younger brother, Wraith, always insisted that Eric come to the city with him, to collect supermodels from the clubs. Eric detested the activity. The girls were like beanbags full of antlers. He had longed for flesh for the longest time, for a real girl that he could really hold on to. Staring at Claire's naked and round form made him harder than steel.

"You don't have to apologize." Claire twisted her nipples between her fingers and sucked her bottom lip between her teeth, biting it gently. "I don't mind if you watch."

Fuck. Where the hell was this coming from?

Eric felt his dick twitching in his trousers. He sat up, a mischievous smile spreading across his face.

"Am I only allowed to watch?"

"You can... touch if you like."

Eric heard the breath racing from his nostrils. He wasn't even using his Intention on the girl, the power that he had to make others do as he wished. This was all her, and hearing the words come from her own lips was making him hornier than anything.

"Well, I suppose it's only fair that I wash you properly before I mate you."

Fear flashed over Claire's face for a moment, but Eric hadn't seen it, because he stood up to strip himself.

"W-What are you doing?" Claire watched, mesmerized, as Eric removed his shirt and pants. A moment later he had rolled down his boxer briefs and was climbing into the tub with her, naked.

"I'm joining you. What does it look like I'm doing?"

Eric lowered himself into the water, barely feeling the heat of it, but enjoying it nonetheless. For the last hundred years, Eric had only known cold. Even the barest fraction of warmth was a pleasure on his skin.

He stretched his legs out under the water, spreading them around Claire's own.

"Give me your hand."

Claire held out her hand as instructed and Eric grabbed it, pulling her across the tub toward him. He wrapped his hands around her waist, cupped her ass in his palms, and pulled her up and onto his thighs. Her warm wetness pressed against the bottom of his shaft. She opened her legs, allowing herself to sit against him more clearly. Eric's cock throbbed with absolute want.

"What are you doing?" Claire sounded afraid. "Are we going...are we going to mate now? Shouldn't we... wait?"

Eric laughed, lowering his head and sucking one of her pink nipples between his teeth. He nibbled at it gently. Claire dropped her head back, moaning at his touch. He felt her fingers fork through his hair and groaned as she pushed her hips against his.

"No." Eric pulled away from her nipple and brought his lips to Claire's. His cock throbbed insistently, urging him to be inside of her. He was relieved that Claire met his kiss with such passion, her entire body melting into his. Eric took a tight grip of her, pulling their bodies together as close as he could while he explored her mouth. He could tell that the young girl wanted nothing more but to sink her pussy down onto his long and rigid shaft, and he wanted nothing more either, but she'd have to wait. "We have to wait." Eric brought his lips to her throat and planted a hot trail of kisses. He wanted nothing more than to turn her, too, but that would have to wait until she was pregnant.

"Why?" She practically moaned the word as she reacted to his pleasurable torment. "Can't we just...please..."

"You've certainly changed your tune." Eric laughed. "Turn around."

Claire did as he asked, turning around in the tub so she was sitting with her back against his chest. Eric's cock steeled as he felt the line of her plump ass touch him. He sat up with his legs on either side of her, holding her own legs open with his hands.

"We have to wait, I have to make sure you're as aroused as possible before I fill you with my seed. That way you will be prepared for mating, and I know your body will be able to take me."

"But—"

"Shh." He drew a finger over her lips as he guided his other hand through the water to the space between her legs. There he found her throbbing pussy and slowly rubbed at her bud, gently putting pressure on it.

Claire opened her mouth and nibbled at his finger. "But I'm so horny now. Please, can't we just fuck?"

"I have to stay away from your pussy until I know you're ready." Eric whispered the words with regret. He wanted nothing more than to be inside of her. Claire kept pushing her ass back and rolling her cheeks against the bottom edge of his shaft. The sensation was driving Eric wild.

"But I *am* ready." Claire moaned as he pushed two fingers inside of her, pulsing them back and forth gently. He moved his other hand to her soap-covered breasts, palming them gently, relishing at how good she felt under his skin.

"You're not." He kept the pad of his thumb on her clit while fucking her with his fingers. An almost constant trickle of groans leapt from her mouth with each breath, making it very hard for Eric to resist her. "You might think you are, but you're not. I'll know when you are."

"But how?" Claire spoke in short gasps now. He pushed the pad of his thumb faster around her clit, slipping his fingers in and out of her cunt deeper and deeper. His hand clamped around her breast, and she brought her hand over his, begging him to squeeze harder. He knew she was nearly there; she was coming.

"Don't worry about that. Just worry about your pleasure for now. I'll let you know once you're there." He craned his head around her, taking her earlobe between his teeth, nibbling at it gently as he fucked her with his hands.

"I-I-I'm there!"

She held him tight as she came, her whole body rocking back and forth in reaction to the orgasm. Water splashed up the sides of the tub, running onto the floor as Claire's body convulsed with pleasure. Eric kept a firm hold of her, feeling ready to blast himself as he felt her pussy clenching around his fingers.

Hearing her gasp in pleasure for him was one of the hottest fucking things that he'd ever heard. He knew that he had to get her worked up so she'd be ready for mating, but he didn't know how much longer *he* could wait. Ever since he had tasted her sweet juices back at her apartment, he'd wanted to be inside of her. She was just too much. Claire turned around to face him and they kissed passionately as her orgasm finished spreading through her with delight.

When he was sure she was done, Eric lay back in the tub with her, running his fingers over her body gently until the water went cold and it was time to climb out.

He stood pitching a tent in the towel wrapped around his waist as he watched Claire dry her curvy body off.

"Come. We will go to the bedroom now." Claire bit her lip at his words and it was all Eric could do to stop himself from ripping her towel off right there. He led Claire out of the bathroom, down the hall, and into the bedroom. She looked around the room in wonder as they entered, equally impressed with the decor in there.

"My goodness," Claire gasped upon seeing the bed, a large round mattress with an exquisitely carved headboard. "Is that where you sleep? That looks amazing."

"Sleep, among many other things. Coffins were never really my thing," Eric joked as he dropped his towel. Claire's eyes lingered on him for a second before looking away. She sat on the bed while Eric dressed himself in fresh clothes: charcoal-colored jeans and a black T-shirt.

"Are you going somewhere?"

"Briefly," Eric answered. "I have to go feed, but I won't be long. I promise."

He saw Claire swallow at his answer. "I'm not going to kill anyone if that's what you're thinking. We have a supply. Don't worry."

"Oh it wasn't that." Claire looked away from him. "I just thought that you might be..."

"...drinking from another woman?"

Claire's face reddened a little.

"It's stupid." She shook her head. "Never mind."

Eric smiled and walked toward her. He placed a hand under her chin and lifted it so she was looking at him.

"The only flesh I ever long to touch now is yours. I would drink from you if I thought I'd be able to stop myself from mating with you. I won't be long."

He turned to walk out the room before turning back to her. "There are clothes for you in the box on the chaise lounge. There's a hairdryer in the bathroom."

Claire nodded. "Thank you. Eric?"

Eric turned back to her.

"Yes?"

"What about anal?"

She twisted the towel between her fingers, finally summoning the strength to look up at him.

Eric swallowed at something in his throat.

"W–What?"

"You said you can't fuck me in my... you know. *Pussy.*"

Just hearing the word on her lips got him hard again.

"But I thought, what about anal? Would that be different?"

Eric's eyebrows raised slowly, betraying his surprise.

Who in heaven is this girl? Lord behold me.

Eric gripped the doorway to steady himself.

"I–I suppose it could be a possibility." The thought hadn't even crossed his mind. But he supposed it might work. He'd have to speak with Ira to make sure it wouldn't ruin the mating ritual. "I won't be long. I promise."

"Take your time." She looked at him with lidded lust, sending another jolt of steel down his cock. "I'll be here, waiting."

CHAPTER THREE

Claire

CLAIRE SAT ALONE IN ERIC'S APARTMENT-LIKE BEDROOM, sitting with her thoughts. The journey to the castle had been hellish. The actual sensation of flight itself was wonderful, but Eric had taken her so high into the sky and they had flown for so long, she was practically frozen by the time they had arrived at Castle Belmont.

The castle was another thing altogether. As they approached she couldn't quite believe her eyes. At first there were only mountains. As they got deeper into the remote range, the first turrets sprang up from the dark hollows of the earth. Endless columns of ancient stone, spires, turrets, and small illuminated windows perched in the stone edifice like a thousand yellow eyes.

She had no idea that anything like that existed, let alone within such close distance of her hometown. There was one peculiar thing that she had noted about the castle: there had been no roads leading to or from it, and it was perched atop a mountain range that overlooked a valley. How on earth did anything get delivered here?

It was a beauty nonetheless. A strange and Gothic beauty, labyrinthine in nature, dark, twisted, mysterious. Claire fell in love with it instantly. By the time they landed, the cold had nearly consumed Claire and it was too much to bear. Shivering in Eric's arms, his demeanor seemed to change immediately. She got the sense that it had been an honest mistake on his behalf, not some cruel torture that he had bestowed upon her with intent.

His regret was evident upon him carrying her inside. "I am sorry. I will warm you immediately."

She had no idea what his words had meant. Perhaps he would get a servant to light some medieval stone fire, a hearth that took up half the room, belting great waves of heat out onto all those that sat in front of it. The wicked part of her mind had hoped for something else. A four-poster bed with intricate rosewood carvings up and down the four pillars. She would be on her back, legs spread, baring herself to him completely. He could be below her, loving her with his mouth again in that amazing way, before pulling his muscled torso up her body and moving himself inside of her.

Neither had been the case however. They had rushed across the rooftop and Claire stared in amazement as his dark expansive wings retreated into his body, folding away like black silk. She had no idea what sort of creature he was really. She used to read vampire books when she was younger, and there were always so many different types between books. She always had a strange fondness for the lore, but when her mother had caught her reading the books she admonished her for it, telling her that such books were the principle literature for "Satan" and that they wouldn't be tolerated in the house of God.

It was just one of the many luxuries that Claire had denied herself in her obstinately inherited faith. She had always been keen to please her mother with her ecclesiastical diligence, but it never seemed to make a difference. Her older sister Lisa — smarter, prettier, skinnier — had always been the apple of her mother and father's eye.

She didn't want any part of her time here at Belmont to surprise her, and if it did, she didn't want to betray it on her face. She would do everything she could to get out of here, and she would do that by making sure Eric was on her side. She wouldn't betray any fear, and she wouldn't betray any horror, no matter how horrific things seemed. She knew that if she wanted to get out of here alive, she would have to gain Eric's trust, and she would do that by making it seem as if she wanted to be here.

Still, watching the strange gargantuan wings disappear into his back, as ghastly as the sight might have seemed to someone else, had almost had no negative effect on her. On the contrary, it only seemed to make Eric more mysterious to her.

His promise of warmth came quickly, and he had carried her through the exquisite hallways of the castle, turning quickly on foot as she clung to him. Within minutes of them landing, he had placed her in a beautiful bronze tub and filled it with hot water and delightfully fragrant soaps. Considering that Eric had painted her tenure here as slavery, this was not the start Claire had anticipated. She had expected chains and dungeons. She had expected cold, pain, misery. When the tub had filled, and the heat came back to her body, she started putting her plan into action. She would try her very best to play along with Eric's games, and she would act as if she were interested.

What surprised Claire the most, however, was how good it felt. She hadn't anticipated Eric would climb in the bath with her, but she was glad that he had. He had a way of bringing pleasure to her body she had never known before. The expert touch of his lips on her breast, the deft strokes of his broad and strong fingers on her sex. Every move he made was with slow and deliberate calculation that only served to heighten her pleasure with every passing moment.

As much as she was convincing herself that she was simply playing along with the game to gain some sort of advantage, it surprised her how much she was enjoying his touch. How much she longed for it when it parted. Even now, sitting on his bed alone in the large room, she had ample opportunity to make an escape, but she couldn't stop drawing up images in her mind of how he'd made her feel.

She felt a sense of shame wash over her again, a leftover from her faith, that all things pleasurable must be scorned and rejected. She didn't want to reject any of this, as much as her mind knew she should. She was aware that back in the apartment, he had controlled her body and her mind somehow, making her want the things that she hadn't. Everything that had happened in the bath had been by her own admission. Claire kept telling herself that she was only playing the game, but even now, barely an hour in, the lines between what she wanted and what she was pretending to want were quickly becoming blurred.

"Stop this." She scorned herself, standing from the bed, pushing the thoughts of Eric out of her mind. She had to keep her mind focused, as much as she wanted the memories of his hands on her body to plague her mind. A shiver passed over her, and she thought it would be a good idea to get dressed.

She walked over to the chaise lounge, where the flat black gloss box sat that Eric had pointed out. She wondered what kind of clothes he had left for her. Upon opening the box, it seemed not very many.

Skimpy black lace lingerie looked up at her. Claire rolled her eyes, almost wanting to smile at the mischievous bastard. With no other option, she slipped the lingerie on and grabbed a plush black robe from off the back of the bedroom door. Eric's room was large and somewhat sprawling. The cold stone floors where covered with an assortment of expensive-looking rugs. The walls were lined with dark and mesmerizing tapestries. On the longest wall of the room there was a long wooden bookshelf, which stretched from ceiling to floor. The shelves were full of ancient-looking tomes, and Gothic objets d'art. Skulls, taxidermy, dozens of half-melted candles. It all looked particularly cliché, but at the same time it fit together extremely well.

There was only one window in the room, another diamond-crossed pane that was set into the stone itself. Claire stood on the balls of her feet, craning her neck to look over the window at the landscape below. Once again, her breath left her at the sight of the beautiful vista. She turned away from the window, quite happy that she had explored the room enough for now, and went into the bathroom to get the hairdryer.

Upon opening the door Claire let out a scream.

Immediately in front of her there was another bronze tub, much like the one she and Eric had been in just a little earlier. In the tub, however, were the bodies of three dead blonde girls.

Her shrill scream filled the air of the room. Her brain told her to run, but her body refused to move, unable to look away from the horrific scene.

They had been stacked in the tub one on top of another, and Claire could see from where she was standing that the bath was half-filled with dark red blood, perfectly still under the flickering light of a candle above her. The girl on the very top barely fit in the crowded vessel, and her left arm was strewn over the edge. Her head lolled over the bathtub edge, her vacant eyes staring directly at the doorway.

Claire turned on her feet and bolted across the apartment, out into the hallway. The stagnant scene was but a chilling reminder that this man wasn't human, he was a demon.

Her feet slapped down cold stone corridors. She couldn't stop the image of the girls from coming back to her, their faces so devoid of color, their eyes so pale and lifeless. And they'd all been naked, as if he'd had his way with them and then drained them when their use was done. Is that what he'd do with her too?

Her breath raced as she fled through the dark hallways. She couldn't believe she had been so naive to even begin to think of trusting him. Everything she had felt for him had been physical, and that was the end of it. She had fallen prey to his wicked black magic, but she wouldn't fall prey to it again, because she was getting out of there.

She rounded a corner and with some relief found herself at the head of a long and winding staircase. She stepped onto the old floral stair-runner and peered over the dark balustrades, eyes hopeful that the stairs descended several flights below. Eric had been very specific to mention that she could move about the floor as she pleased, but not to venture into the lower parts of the castle. She hesitated for a moment, remembering his words, only for them to be replaced by the image of the three dead girls.

"No. He lies. He can't be trusted." She gripped the dark wood of the staircase and descended the steps as fast as her feet could take her. Whatever lay in the castle below, surely it couldn't be any worse than the murderer with whom she had inhabited.

She flew down the stairs, all the while casting glances behind her, afraid she would see Eric standing there, arms crossed, looking at her as if her escape attempt was nothing more than a mere infraction. She knew that if she didn't get out of there, she would end up just the same as those girls. She knew that his words had been nothing but lies. She played their last conversation in her mind, as she descended deeper and deeper into the castle. He'd said he didn't hunt; he said he'd never touch another's flesh again. At the time she'd dared to believe it, but that was just the naivety of her post-coital brain. To think she'd even proffered the idea of anal intercourse with the man?

What was she thinking?

It was the part that Claire hated most about this whole ordeal. That even when she was acting with her own intentions, she wasn't acting like herself. She wasn't the type of girl to fuck strange men in bathtubs, and offer them *anal sex* as an afterthought. Right now, running for her life, she had no idea why she'd even thought to offer such a thing. His effect on her had been so maddening at the time that she'd wanted nothing more than just to feel him inside of her. No. Clearly it wasn't her own intention that she was acting with. He was still bewitching her somehow, just another sign that he couldn't be trusted and she had to leave.

Claire reached the bottom of the tall staircase and glanced out of the first window she came across. To her disappointment she was still hundreds of feet up in the air. Peering over the lower sill of the window, she could just make out the curling edifice of the castle wall, swooping down toward the ground that was so very far away.

"Fuck!" She spat her frustration in a whisper, infuriated that the staircase couldn't just get her down to the ground floor. Eric had mentioned earlier that they were on the ninth floor, and it had seemed that was at the top of the castle. She'd definitely just gone down more than nine flights. What in hell's name was wrong with this place?

Suddenly, the sound of a door opening came from down the corridor. Claire glanced in terror in the direction of the noise. She was standing directly in the middle of the corridor, plain for all to see. She spun back to face the staircase from which she'd just descended. No, she wouldn't go back to him. To go back now would mean certain death. She turned and ran down the corridor, in the opposite direction of the noise.

Large and sealed doors flanked her on both sides. Up ahead she could see light from the right-hand side of the passage. An open door, a room perhaps in which she could hide until it was clear for her to come out again.

As she approached the door she peered carefully around its frame and saw a large and open library. She quickly looked to the broad and tall windows at the back of the library, which illuminated the entire room with a gentle pallor. The room seemed empty. She would have to take a chance.

Footsteps floated from the corridor behind her. Claire glanced back, knowing that whoever they belonged to would see her within a second if she didn't move fast.

She darted into the library, closing both the doors behind her as gently as possible. It was only upon turning to face the room that she stood face-to-face with an impossibly tall and broad man, who was smiling down on her wickedly.

"Eric?!"

"Well, well, well. What have we here?"

He closed the distance between them completely with one stride, forcing Claire against the door as he did so. He smoothed the back of his hand down the right side of her face. His dark crimson eyes burned like fire.

"I was just exploring," Claire whimpered. "I got lost. Please take me back to your room Eric."

"Eric?" The vampire laughed. "I'm afraid you've mistaken me for my brother. Speaking of which... you smell like him." He leaned in, inhaling Claire's scent, with no regard for her personal space whatsoever. "It's foul. But I'll get that scent off you soon. Don't you worry."

"I don't understand." Claire looked into the blood-red eyes of the man she had thought was Eric. Staring closely, she realized it wasn't him, but they looked almost identical. He had the same chiseled features, the same strong jawline. The hair was long and wild however, and his nose was slightly longer and more narrow. "If you're not Eric, who are you?"

"Wraith," he answered with an evil smile, brushing a finger over Claire's lips.

Claire shook her head, terrified. Whatever this strange beast was, she got the sense that he was something much worse than Eric. A chill rose in the pit of her stomach, and she realized she was filled with utter dread.

"No..." she whispered. "Please."

His hands were on her wrists, and he tore her from the door with inhuman strength. The sheer momentum of his force caused her feet to stumble across the floor. They carried her into the library until she crashed into a table, tumbling over it with a large grunt. He was behind her in a flash, moving with inhuman speed. The barbed sting of his crotch pushed against her legs, and his hands smoothed over her robe. He tore the robe from her with one swift movement, revealing the lingerie underneath.

"Very nice." His words sounded more like snarling than anything else. Claire's whole body trembled underneath her as the brute smoothed his hands over her flesh, pulling at the edges of her lingerie.

"You're so *very* scared. Are you running from something? Was Eric hunting you?" Wraith laughed. "It's not like Eric to hunt. Still... it's not like him to keep slaves either. You're a little larger than I like, but I guess you have a pretty face. I almost want to keep you for a while, but..."

She felt his hands clutch around her panties, tearing them apart, exposing her to him completely. "It will annoy him so much more if I rape and kill you. That'll teach him to let his pets run around like stray dogs."

"No, please...no!" Claire stammered, her voice quivering, protesting, shaking. She knew it was no good.

She heard his trousers drop and felt a cold flat hand pushing on her shoulder blades, forcing her down onto the table.

"Quiet," he growled with a wicked whisper. "I'm having my playtime now."

CHAPTER FOUR

Eric

ERIC SAT THERE STARING AT IRA'S OFFICE IDLE-EYED, as the doctor moved about the room like a sundrenched sloth. Ira had been a doctor in his early pre-vampire life, and he had kept his office like it was still the late 1800s, from the white tiles on the walls to the rough and uncomfortable leather green stools in the waiting area. Next to the clinical shine of the stainless-steel cart and the precise glass vials filled with dark red blood, the room looked at odds with itself.

Ira was the chief doctor for the Belmont family, as he had been for the past several hundred years. He was also the botanist, architect, painter, sartorialist... he was a man of many interests, and with the luxury of eternal life, he'd had plenty of time to indulge in them, filling his mind with an impressive expanse of knowledge, not just of things human, but things vampire too.

He was also of a class of vampires that now took time for granted, as he had all the time in the world to himself. He moved at a pace that was lackadaisical, reminiscent of a shadow crawling across a wide garden on a long summer afternoon.

Eric watched the man, while squeezing his fingers around the hard edge of the leather-clad stool. Unlike many of the other vampires at Castle Belmont, Eric did have an air of patience about him, something he had learned while growing up underneath his maliciously stubborn father. If kept too long from simple pleasures like blood or sex, vampires would quickly become short and agitated.

Ira didn't tolerate impatience, and anyone who dared to push him quickly found themselves on the end of his sharp tongue. He took no time in reminding anyone who cared to complain that the service he was providing to them was a benefit, not a luxury, and he could withdraw it anytime he wished.

Eric had never complained; unlike others he was grateful for the service that Ira provided. Over the last few years Eric's taste for the hunt had dissipated, replaced only by the constant and irremovable thirst for blood. He'd tried to wean himself from the dark nectar, but found it next to impossible. Reducing his usual intake by even the barest fraction brought out splitting headaches and agonizing lethargy across his whole body.

He hadn't hunted a real person in almost three years, and even then, he'd done so with much reluctance. He'd been traveling across Europe on business for the family when the supply in their trailer had been damaged in a storm. There were always networks, always places a well-known vampire like a Belmont could go to get blood. But even in the deadest remote areas of ancient Europe, Eric was loath to find he had reached an impasse. He'd resorted to taking to a small village, and in the dead of the night, he abducted a young girl. Perhaps only twenty. He'd tried to take just enough to keep him going, just enough to let her live. In his mind he knew that she had died, however, even though he hadn't stuck around to see the outcome.

Since then he'd been especially careful to keep stocks of blood, and he was paramount in helping Ira develop the blood stores within the castle. A special wing had been constructed underground, which was climate-controlled and protected by a number of backup generators. Blood of all types was kept, although if Eric was honest with himself he could never taste the difference. The key difference was the person: younger was better. But not too young. An adult in their prime was best, and he had a preference for women, but everyone was different.

His dependency on blood was another tome of walking shame for him. Every meal was a disappointment. An essential and invigorating disappointment.

"You seem on edge today, Master Belmont." Ira puttered about gathering supplies, casting a wry smile in Eric's direction.

Eric steeled his jaw, took a deep breath, and tried to remind himself that patience was important with Ira. Normally he could bear to wait, even when the shadows within him were screaming out for sustenance. Today, however, his patience was almost nonexistent. He craved something even greater than blood, and if he hadn't been scared he might do something stupid with Claire in blood thirst, he would have skipped this meal altogether.

He wanted the girl, and he wanted her badly. He wanted her so badly that it surprised him. He was Eric Belmont. The immortal bachelor, the heir to the Belmont empire. He didn't have time for girls, and he certainly didn't have time for *love.* There had been times in the past, decades ago, when he thought he might have loved slaves, but it had always just turned out to be deep-rooted lust.

Slaves were just things at the end of the day, and things always got broken in Castle Belmont, especially with a brother like Wraith running around. Eric wasted no time getting upset over it; he'd long since accepted it as a fact of life. He'd find a new slave, drink from her for a while, and then he'd come home one day to find her dead or broken after Wraith had had his wicked way with her.

Eric had never understood the young lunatic he was forced to call a brother. Eric never saw sense in torture, never saw pleasure in mindless murder. These were the things his brother thrived upon however, and he had murdered so many of Eric's slaves on purpose, just to get a rise out of him. There might have been a time when it worked, but it had been a long time since Eric could remember his brother's escapades really getting to him. He didn't hold any ill will against his brother; ultimately he knew that it wasn't his fault. He just wished there was something he could do to change him.

He'd barely had Claire twenty-four hours, and already he could feel something changing within him, a change that was greater than any he had known in his three hundred years. It scared him, and it excited him at the same time.

He *wanted* Claire. He wanted her all to himself. To be away from her for even just a few minutes felt like pain. As soon as he was done with Ira, he'd take an extra supply of blood for the weekend, and he'd hole himself up in the room with his new obsession. His mind was hell-bent on one thing, and that was delivering as much pleasure to her as possible over the next few days. Even if the act hadn't served the purpose of making their inevitable mating more effective, he would have partaken in it gladly. He cast his mind over the bath they had shared just some time ago, groaning inwardly as his cock grew in his pants. He thought about the softness of her nipples, the firmness of her ass. How pale and beautiful her skin was. How her pussy had felt when he had cupped it in his hand.

His cock turned to steel, pushing against the tight fabric of his jeans. He shifted in the seat, leather squeaking beneath him as he did so.

"And you're usually so much more chatty."

Eric looked up to see that Ira was standing in front of him. He'd been in such deep thought over Claire he'd completely forgotten he was in the room. In front of Ira was the stainless steel cart, which had Eric's dose on it for the morning.

"Two pints. Renal, duogenarian. This is a really good one." Ira took a small shot glass from off the counter and supped at it. Eric blinked hard, breathing his frustration out. Ira had a penchant for flourish. Sometimes he wished the man would just speak normally. *Blood from the kidneys of a twenty-year-old.* That's all his blather had meant. He smiled at the doctor politely, taking a pint from the counter, and finished it quickly.

"My, someone *is* hungry." Ira stared at him wide-eyed. Eric ignored the comment, grabbed the second pint, and drank from the glass deeply. He set the glass back on the metal cart and wiped his hand across the back of his mouth. He glanced at Ira, and saw the man was staring down at him with a squinting suspicion.

"What are you up to today? It's not like you to be in a rush, and I know rush when I see it."

"Nothing." Eric stood up, stretching his stiff body in his clothes. "I just have things that I need to do. Stuff for the family. You know what's it like."

Ira nodded his head as if he did know. "Heir of Belmont, transformative times, succession of power to a younger and more powerful vampire... lots to do I suppose." Ira spoke in long and rambling sentences, which were hard to keep up with for those unfamiliar with his cadence. To Eric, it was nothing too hard; he'd kept the company of the man for several decades now.

"Yes, well." Eric started for the door. "I have to be off now."

"Very busy it would seem," Ira said with curious remark.

Eric stopped, recalling the last words he had shared with Claire. The delicious and enticing words that had his cock on end nearly all morning. He turned back to Ira, the man who had more knowledge than any other in Castle Belmont, and he cleared his throat.

"Ira. I was wondering. You know when a vampire is with a breeder?"

"Human?"

"Yes. It's known that arousal should be at peak levels before consummation..."

"Yes, in order to fully make sure the breeder is ready." Ira recited the words as if reading from an old medical book.

"Well. What about..." Eric almost flushed in the cheeks at the absurdity of the question. "What about anal sex? Would that disturb the readiness or..."

He faded off, hoping that the bulk of the brief question had been significant enough.

A curious smile spread across Ira's face and he shook his head.

"What *are* you up to up there, Master Belmont? I do wonder sometimes... but no. To answer your question, I don't believe that would have any adverse effect on the breeding process. In fact, I think it would work quite on the contrary, in heightening the breeder's arousal."

Eric's eyes widened in excitement. "Really?"

"Oh yes. I remember reading an entry in the Belmont family archives. The diary of Belladonna Vandark."

"Belladonna? She's not of our line." Eric's ears turned at the name. Belladonna Vandark. Her name was an infamous one. While most vampires knew a generous amount of sexual deviancy, Belladonna Vandark was on a whole other level.

"No, you're right. But there was a time in the early 1900s when I was an archivist for their family. When I left I still had a lot of their effects in my possession for one reason or another. It sat in storage for years, but I decided to put it in the Belmont archives. I have let Belladonna know, but she seems to care little."

"She probably hardly remembers." Eric laughed. It had been many years since he had met the woman, and she was barely a name on his radar, but he knew that she had grown reclusive and distant to the vampire world in the last century.

"She found herself a male breeder, and she had quite the penchant for anal sex, documenting it thoroughly in her journal."

"I bet," Eric quipped. "But thanks... that's all I need to know."

"Anything *I* need to know?" Ira rocked onto his tiptoes, holding his arms behind him, neck craned out.

"Nothing as of yet, Doctor. Thanks for the blood."

"Anytime, Eric. Anytime."

Eric turned to leave before stopping once more. "And Doctor. Could you send up three days' worth of supply to my room?"

Ira's eyebrows raised slowly. "We really are busy, hmm? But yes. I can't see why not. I'll have one of the servants leave it in your personal cooler."

Eric nodded and flew from the room quickly.

*

There was a reason for Eric keeping Claire's presence at the castle secret. Breeders like Claire were rare, and for him to find one was something of a treasure. The political climate in Castle Belmont had always been testy. Their line was one of the most powerful, and one of the most respected families on the occidental side of the vampire world. His father, Atticus

Belmont, was the current head of the family crest, but his time was coming to an end and he was preparing to hand over the reins.

There had been many decades of subterfuge, conspiracy, and collusion to try and manipulate the passing of power, but Atticus had done a good job of keeping order within the castle. Things were set to pass to Eric. There were several brothers and uncles, and even aunts, that would like to take the throne, but Atticus had managed to satiate their thirst for power by giving them power in far and distant places. It was a brilliant strategy that had worked for the most part. The only vampires left in the castle itself were the ones suspected to have no ulterior motives, no desire to usurp or scramble desperately for power when the chance presented itself.

Eric knew better. As much as he and his father had tried to clean the castle of filth, it was always wise to watch one's back. Eric's claim for inheritance was already a strong one. He was the oldest heir, he was respected, and he was powerful. His younger brother for the most part accepted this, but his brother Wraith was a problem, as he was in all facets of life. Eric knew that Wraith would accept the passing of power, but he knew that he was also conspiring to overthrow him as soon as he could.

With the ability to produce an heir, Eric had a distinct advantage over his brother and sisters, who as of yet, had no means to reproduce themselves. Before claiming her, Claire would be fair game to any vampire who wanted her. This is why it was important for Eric to mate and turn her as fast as possible. After the initial mating, he would be bonded to her and he could turn her. Turning her before that would negate her breeding ability. Upon turning, Claire would be a fertile vampire, an extreme rarity, and one that would be respected by every vampire in the world. It would bring power, and it would bring advantage.

However great the political advantages of having an heir, they were the last on the list of Eric's motivations for taking Claire. Eric couldn't care less about securing his inheritance of the throne. His first and greatest motivation had been just to have an heir; a child was what he had wanted more than anything in the world. But even this had slipped now, pushed under the ebb and flow of the pure carnal desire that he felt for Claire and the desire he felt to keep her safe.

He rushed back to his room with great haste, and when he got there, he was terrified to see that Claire was gone.

"Claire?"

Eric walked around the room quickly, his eyes scanning in every direction.

"Claire, it's Eric. Where are you?"

The lack of response stirred torment in Eric's chest. He stood for a moment, listening, clenching his fists in angst, squeezing his nails into the palms of his hands.

He cast his eyes all around the room, from the bed in front of him to the study on the right and back to the bathroom on the left.

The bathroom.

He had told her the hairdryer was in there. He noticed she'd removed the lingerie from the box on the chaise lounge. Just the thought of seeing her in it got him hard again. He stalked across room to the en-suite, and pushed the door open.

He saw the bodies of the three naked girls in the tub and turned from the scene immediately, pushing his hand into the bridge of his nose.

Wraith.

That cretinous bastard. The last time he had seen him was just before he'd left for the city, to collect Claire. He'd passed Wraith in a corridor in the original part of the castle.

"In a hurry, brother? I've left a surprise for you in your wing. You'll find it, I'm sure."

He'd cackled with brazen inanity as Eric had pushed past him. He was used to his brother's games, but there had been no time to pay him any attention. This must have been the surprise that Wraith had mentioned. Three young women, dead in his personal bathroom. Murdered simply for the pleasure of briefly entertaining Wraith. Eric's body shook with rage. He knew instantly what had happened. Claire must have found the bodies, and she must have assumed that they were Eric's. Why wouldn't she? They were in his bathroom after all.

She must have run. She was obviously somewhere in the castle. Eric knew that it was impossible for her to escape. There was no way out of the castle on foot, so she must be inside it somewhere, hiding. Blood thundered through his temples as he stood, chest heaving, contemplating how to find her.

He closed his eyes and took a deep breath. There was a connection between them, no matter how faint. If he could tune everything out and focus on her, there was a possibility he might be able to find her.

He drew another deep breath, tasting the air of the castle. Dust, varnish, wood, leather. These were all things that were a permanence in the air of Belmont. He sought past that, looking further. There was a trace of her on the air, a trace of her delicious floral sent, tinged with fright. He could almost taste her fear, the way she had felt when she had seen the bodies.

She had left the room in a hurry, turned down the corridor, and headed in the direction of the southeast staircase. Eric ran, following the scent quickly. It was then that the second sight hit him. He froze in the corridor, steadying himself against a stone wall with his hand as his eyes glazed over.

He saw the bodies, he felt her fear. She had turned quickly and ran. She ran the length of the corridor, until she came to the staircase.

No, Eric begged in his mind, even though he knew he was only watching a trace of something that had already been.

She took the stairs, she ran quickly and quietly, all the way to the bottom, until she reached the twelfth floor. His floor. Wraith's floor.

No.

He heard the sound of a door opening, and then the vision faded away.

Eric ran at once, moving down the corridor with great speed. Claire had wandered onto one of the most dangerous floors in the castle, the floor of his twisted and insane brother, Wraith. If Wraith found Claire before Eric did, it wouldn't be long until she was dead.

Eric turned at the stairs, launching down the flight in one swift jump. He kicked his foot off the wall on the landing and launched in the opposite direction down the next flight, moving like this until he was at the bottom.

He could sense her completely now. She had turned right, down the corridor, heading in the direction of the library. She wasn't alone, however. Wraith was in there too.

*

As soon as Eric threw open the great doors of the library, he saw his brother standing naked, Claire doubled over in front of him, her lingerie ripped to shreds. Upon hearing the doors Wraith looked over his shoulder with an expression of fury etched on his face, indignant that someone would dare disturb his playtime.

To Claire, everything that happened in those next three seconds was an imperceptible blur of noise and movement.

To Eric however, the movement was swift and keen preciseness. He launched from the door to his brother's place with inhuman speed. Wraith turned to meet his brother, matching his speed. The fury that had been on his face slipped to fear, and immediately he could sense that some line had been crossed. Wraith threw his arms up to block his brother's attack, but he wasn't fast enough to match the rage that was driving Eric forward.

Eric launched up into the air, turning his body forward as he did so, until he was above Wraith with his hands pointed down at him. He seized him by the jaw and held tight. Eric continued to soar through the library, his body turning as he did so, until he was upright once more. At the end of his first revolution he let his brother's head slip from his grasp, launching his body across the remainder of the library until it crashed into the windows at the far end of the room.

Claire stood dazed. Just one moment ago Wraith had been behind her, his cold hands groping at her body. He had been mere seconds from raping her. Now he was in front of her, at the far end of the library in a twisted heap on the ground. Between them was Eric, standing on a table looking down at his brother.

Wraith flung himself to his feet. To Claire this was another blur of movement. To Eric he saw every part of the motion.

"Come to play, brother?! Finally!" A wild smile spread across Wraith's face, eager that Eric had finally risen to his challenge.

Eric had no time for games. Wraith had come *this* close to taking away the one thing in the world that was important to him. Wraith wanted some long drawn-out fight, some dramatic dance where bodies would be heaved through pillars of stone and dust. Eric didn't care for it. He could have thrown him harder and launched him through the windows into the pure daylight. He could have ignited the fool and ended it once and for all. He hadn't, however.

"Come on, Eric!" Wraith's eyes shrank to pinpricks. The whites were large and fevered. "Fight me!"

Wraith launched himself at Eric, anticipating that this was all just some roughhousing. Eric intercepted Wraith by the throat, driving back through the air to the window once more. His body crunched against the glass. Eric moved with his full strength and speed, using the full capacity of his power that he rarely showed to anyone. It took Wraith by surprise, and his eyes were shrunken in fear now.

"Hark, brother!" Wraith writhed under Eric's grasp, his hand uncomfortably tight on his throat. "She's just a slave! Relax!"

Eric tightened his grip further, just seconds away from feeling the trachea of his brother's throat collapse in his fingers.

"No." His voice was low and wild.

Wraith tried to wriggle free, but his brother's strength was too much. "Enough! You can have her! It was just a joke!"

"If you ever touch her again, I'll stake you myself."

Wraith laughed at the words at first, but then his face turned ghostly white, seeing that his brother was not joking.

Eric held Wraith like that for a few seconds more, unable to relax at the idea of him being in the same room with Claire. Finally he relented and lowered him back down, taking a step back.

Wraith straightened himself out, cockiness flooding back into his face now that he was free.

"Not worth killing anyway," Wraith spat. "Much more fun to torture girls like *that*."

In a split second Eric grabbed a chair beside him, slammed it onto the floor, and thrust Wraith up against the wall once more with a splintered leg held against his chest.

"This is your last warning. I will stake you myself. If you ever touch, talk, or think about her again, I will kill you. Is that understood?"

Wraith's whole body shook under Eric's grasp.

"Is that understood?"

"Yes!" he snarled reluctantly. "Now get off me!"

Eric dropped the stake, and with a twisting motion he launched his brother back through the air of the library, toward the main doors. Wraith landed on his feet with ease, staring back at his brother skittishly.

"Leave."

"This is my floor!"

"*Leave.*"

He pushed the word out of his throat with the whispered fire of rage. Wraith sensed he was mere seconds from final death and tore from the library, roaring in frustration as he fled down the corridor.

Eric took a few breaths to steady his fury, and then his eyes were back on Claire, who stood cowering in the corner, her arms twisted in front of her naked body. He was in front of her in a second, holding the discarded bathrobe that had been dropped onto the floor. He held the robe out and Claire snatched it from his hand, jumping away from him as she covered her body.

"Please! Just let me go! Please! Don't kill me!"

"My dearest Claire." He placed a hand on her waist and another on the side of her face, brushing his lips softly across her forehead. "I will protect you with my life."

"I saw the bodies," she stammered. "I saw what you did!"

"That was my brother's doing." He pushed reassurance from the depth of his chest, soothing her fear. Slowly but surely her breath calmed, until she could look up at him once more.

"No, but...it was, your—"

"Wraith has often been a thorn in my side. I told you that I don't hunt anymore, and that was the truth. You have nothing to fear."

A glimpse of hope seemed to spark in her eyes again, if only for the barest of seconds. Eric could use his full Intention on her if he wanted. He could turn her into a slobbering drone that said yes and obeyed without hesitation. He didn't want that though. He wanted *her*, and if he wanted to gain her trust he had to do it the hard way.

"Promise it to me," she said, breath shaking. "Promise me that it wasn't you."

Eric spoke immediately without hesitation. "I promise you. Now promise me something."

Claire turned her head in curiosity.

"Promise me that you believe me."

Claire's eyes looked down, then back up at Eric, and then around the library. She weighed his words with deep consideration. After what felt like an eternity, she finally spoke.

"Look into my eyes and tell me it wasn't you," she said.

Eric did as she said. Claire swallowed at his words.

"I believe you," she said.

"Really?"

"Yes. I can tell. Just looking at you. You're fierce, for sure. You're strong... but you're different. You're not him. You're not your brother. He's... he's ghastly."

"Agreed." Eric laughed briefly and his smiled faded. "I apologize for our rocky start. Come." He offered his hand out for Claire to take it. She looked at it, hesitating. "I'll have Ira clean up the mess. I'll take you back to safety."

"I can't. I can't go back there," she stammered.

"I wouldn't dream of it, my love. That was but one of my many rooms. I have another, on the opposite corner of the castle. It's even nicer actually. A little modern for my tastes, but I think you will like it. Will you come?"

Her eyes had been in the distance, looking at something out of sight, probably playing back the dark images of the bodies. He placed a finger on her chin and pulled at it for her to look at him.

She did, and a slight smile crossed her lips.

"Will you come? I promise this is the last horror you will see here. Everything else..."

He brushed his hand down her neck, skirting the circumference of her breast. "Everything else will be pleasure."

Claire swallowed.

"Did you find out?"

Eric turned his head in confusion.

"...about the thing that we talked about," Claire said, abashed, color filling her cheeks. Eric realized what she meant immediately.

"Ah." A smile spread across his face. "Yes I did. And yes. It should be perfectly fine." He held his hand out once more.

"Come. We have all that to look forward to and more. I promise, you won't regret it."

She placed her hand in his. Eric breathed a sigh of relief. She was his once again. He walked her out of the library, back toward the staircase, back to the ninth floor.

As they walked he bit his lip in anticipation. He had her all to himself again, and he wouldn't be letting her go anytime soon.

CHAPTER FIVE

Claire

CLAIRE FELT THANKFUL FOR ERIC'S PROTECTION, but she also felt dread. She had looked upon Eric as a savior, and after seeing how he'd dealt with his twisted brother Wraith, it only cemented that feeling. Then she had felt the apprehension again, remembering the bodies of the girls in the bathroom. Somehow, he had managed to find a way to make her feel better.

Once she understood that it had been his brother, and not Eric, who had left the bodies in the bathroom, she breathed a sigh of relief. Maybe her dark captor wasn't that dark after all? It was bizarre, but just being in the presence of Eric made her feel safe again. Claire walked with Eric, torn between three separate emotions. There was the desire to stay with her beautiful and mysterious captor, there was the desire to slap herself stupid, and the desire to leave the castle. No matter how safe Eric made her feel, the castle and its inhabitants were a danger to her. Claire felt like stepping outside her own body, taking herself by the shoulders and shaking them violently.

This place will be the end of you, her mind screamed. *Leave now before it's too late!*

She shushed the voices, pushing them to the back of her mind. She half-convinced herself that she still wanted to escape, and that she was only humoring Eric by following him. The bodies, the psychopathic brother—it was all terrifying, but the part that scared Claire the most was how she *wanted* to risk her own life by staying here, even if just to be with Eric for a little longer.

"Come," he said as he guided her through the dark hallways. They were back on his floor now, but it was a part that she hadn't seen before. Eric walked just ahead of her. He looked back and saw the fear on her face.

"Have no worries, Claire. We won't return to that old room." He took her hand and squeezed it for reassurance.

Claire was somewhat surprised the gesture worked.

"Where are we going," Claire asked, "if not your room?"

"I have another room on the southwest corner of the castle."

"Two rooms?" Claire laughed. "You're spoiled rotten. Mr. Belmont."

He looked back at her, his blood-red eyes twinkling with mischief. "Now that I have you, everything before was a mere shadow."

They turned down a hallway and Eric led her through a door into another bedroom. It was decidedly Gothic, much like his other room, but this one was certainly more modern with its furnishings.

On the far wall there was a long window that ran nearly the whole width of the room, which was a covered in a long black blind that blocked out the light.

Eric walked into the room, peeling away from Claire.

"Bed, bathroom, TV... all the facilities you could ever want."

"Do vampires watch a lot of TV?" Claire giggled.

"Not me." He walked to the sleek bedside cabinet and opened its black drawer, pulling out an e-reader.

"Lifesaver. Every book I've ever read is on here."

"I thought you said vampires and technology don't get along?" Claire said, sitting down on the bed beside him.

"We don't usually, but I've never had a problem with this thing. The more basic, the better things tend to be." He nodded at the large flat screen TV in the far corner. "That thing tends to work as long as I keep my distance. I'm not really much of a TV person."

"Me neither," Claire said, glancing up at his face and relishing his beauty.

Eric placed his e-reader back in the drawer, closing it. "Bathroom is over there, and—"

He stopped speaking, upon seeing Claire's reaction to his words.

Claire stared in the direction of the bathroom. The sleek black door stood slightly ajar, giving the barest glimpse of the dark tiles within.

She felt something clasp her back, and looking down she was surprised to see it was Eric's hand. He brought a finger to her face and pulled at it so she was looking at him.

"Look at me. There's nothing in there."

He stood, walked across the room to the en suite door, and turned the light on. He looked inside.

"Come. I promise you."

Claire took a deep breath and walked across the room, pausing a moment before looking around the door at the empty bathroom.

"I'm the only person in the house that has a key to this place. It's just me and you in here, no one else, I promise. You don't have to be afraid in here. You're safe now."

"I'm not afraid," Claire said honestly. "It was just a shock seeing them, that's all. I worked in the hospital for two years. I've seen dead bodies before, plenty of them. It wasn't seeing the bodies that shocked me, it was the thought that…"

She broke off, realizing that the end of her sentence might cause offense.

"The thought that I had done it?" Eric nodded solemnly. "It's okay, you can say that. I'd given you just cause to think that way. I was a tad bit wicked with you on our first meeting, and for that I apologize."

They walked from the bathroom to the bed and sat.

"Am I making you mellow out, Mr. Belmont?" Claire bit her lip, teasing Eric.

Eric flashed a flirtatious grin back in her direction and Claire felt her stomach flip. "I must admit, you seem to have some sort of mellowing effect on me. As far as vampires go, I like to think of myself as one of the more *decent* ones. There are plenty of vampires out there like my brother, Wraith. Some even worse. Vampires who run amok, killing everything that they desire without so much as thinking of the consequences."

Claire's throat tightened at the thought. Worse than Wraith? But he was already so maniacal…

"A funny word to use," Eric said.

Claire looked up at him, shocked, and then realized that he had read her thoughts again.

"I'd like it if you stopped doing that." Claire said. "Reading my thoughts."

The faintest trace of pink seemed to etch across Eric's ivory-white cheeks. Had she just made him blush?

"Are you giving me orders, Ms. Eldridge?"

His voice was cold and flat, tinged with a seriousness that brushed fear across Claire's body. She ignored the intimidation and looked past it however, realizing that there was more to him than just boyish threat. He was ashamed of what he'd done.

"And what if I am? If you're going to snatch me out of my home and bring me here, then there are rules that I'm laying down. Especially if you want to stand a chance of putting a baby inside of me."

Claire sat up straight, and tried with utmost intent to make her voice sound authoritative. There were points when it broke, and points when it sounded shaky, but for the most part she was pleased with her delivery. She had no idea how Eric would react, and she had no idea where this resolve was coming from, but something was driving her to put a pin in her corner.

"Very well." Eric said, the faintest hint of a smile pulling up at his lips. "What are these rules, Ms. Eldridge?"

His eyes flicked down to her body for a moment and he moved his hand across her thigh, stroking his palm down toward her knee ever so slowly.

The motion nearly derailed Claire completely, his soft fingers sending tingling sparks up and down her leg, which fizzled at the top across her groin and up the sides of her sex.

"Well, I—" she stammered, hating how much he could turn her on with just a touch. She grabbed his hand and placed it on the mattress, standing up so she was facing him.

"I want you to stop reading my mind. It's not fair that you can read my mind and I can't read yours. You know all my deepest darkest secrets if you want to. Why should you be the one who gets to know everything? It's not fair."

"Okay," Eric said.

"And second of all, stop using your voice to make me do things…" She lingered on the word for a moment.

"Things?" Eric asked, chuckling.

"You know very well what I mean!" Claire looked around, not wanting to explain verbally. "Sexy things! You know. Stop making me do all that, it's not fair!"

"Well, I only used a little of my Intention, and that was back at your apartment. Everything since then has been you, my darling."

The admission stopped Claire in her tracks. "Wait, what?"

"Yes, I used a little to open you up and make you relax, but I only drew on desires that were already inside of you. Everything else has been just you, my sweet."

"But, the bath, the library…"

"All you," Eric said, eyes twinkling. "I don't like using Intention much; it almost feels like cheating."

"What is that?" Claire asked. "That word you keep using. Intention. Is that what it's called?"

"That's what we call it," Eric answered. "Others have other names for it. Most vampires possess some form of Intention, but it's stronger in some than others."

"Intention, that's what it's called when you use your voice to make people do things?"

Eric nodded. "I already told myself I wouldn't use it on you anymore. It's too easy to *make* people like me. I don't want to do that with you. I want *you* to like me, not for you to feel like you *have* to."

"I don't feel like that," Claire said quickly, afraid that she might have offended him somehow.

"I promise I'll stop reading your thoughts. You're right; it's not fair for me to do so. Was there anything else?"

"I don't know," Claire said honestly. "I'd only thought about those two. I feel like I have a million questions I want to ask you about being a vampire, but I don't want to load it all on you at once."

"That's all right." Eric smiled. "It's perfectly normal to be curious. Was there anything you wanted to know in particular?"

Claire thought for a moment.

"This place, you live here with your family?"

Eric nodded.

"Are there vampires everywhere?"

He shrugged.

"We don't know. We know some things, we know of others, but we don't know everything. There are parts of being a vampire that are as mysterious to me as they are to you."

Claire walked back to the bed, sitting down beside Eric. She leaned against his body and he wrapped his arm around her.

"And what about Wraith?"

She felt his hand tense at the mention of his brother's name.

"What about him?"

"What's his story, why is he that way?"

She heard Eric take a deep breath and sigh. "There are reasons for my brother's... behavior. Reasons that you will come to learn in time. It's not for us to discuss now, however. Let us move on from dark mentions of my brother for now. Let us focus on lighter things."

"I'm sorry," Claire said with a rasping whisper. She hadn't noticed now until she'd sat down in Eric's arms, but she was so dreadfully tired, so dreadfully exhausted. She sat up a little, yawning, stretching her body.

"You know, I hadn't realized until now, but I haven't slept since you took me."

Eric looked down at her hands in his lap.

"I apologize," he said. "I've been a pretty dreadful host. I haven't slept either—how about we take rest together? We can come back to everything else tonight."

Before Claire realized what was happening, Eric had brought her a pair of black satin pajamas. She changed into them, marveling at their comfort. He stripped down to charcoal-gray boxers, and Claire tried her hardest not to gawk at his exquisite body. His body almost seemed to glow in the dim light of the room. As she lay on the bed, she watched his silhouette move around the room. The light caught on the tight muscles of his body, highlighting his pecs and abdominals. Just above the line of his underwear Claire could see the outline of his Adonis belt, the arrow of muscle that pointed down to the well-stuffed underwear that sat at the top of his muscled thighs.

"And what about the rest of your family?" Claire mused as he slipped under the covers next to her. She gasped upon feeling the warmth of his crotch pressing against her rear as he held her from behind. His hand slipped around her, resting gently over hers.

She felt safe and secure in his embrace.

"In the castle?" His voice whispered over her ear like black velvet.

"Yes..." Claire nodded, her voice starting to become lulled by sleep.

"There's my father, and my two sisters. Veronica and Sophia. Then there's Wraith and me. That's all."

"No mother?"

"No." Eric paused. "Not anymore."

*

Claire was in a midnight forest, staring up at the oak branches high above her, listening as they creaked in the night wind.

"You'll catch your death in the cold out here."

She turned slowly to face the voice. He stepped from the shadows of an ink-black tree, walking until his arms were around her.

"How did you find me out here?" she whispered, staring at the ethereal beauty that was his face.

Light itself seem to emanate from his ivory complexion, illuminating the darkness like an angel.

"I can always find you," he said, pressing his soft red lips against hers.

Claire moaned into his mouth. She closed her eyes, letting her whole body relax in his strong embrace. He drew his lips from her and placed them onto her throat, suckling at her flesh, long and deep.

"You bewitch me," she gasped.

He guided a hand down between her legs, pulling the hem of her dress up, probing at the silky softness between her thighs.

"Oh Eric..." Her head lolled as he slipped a finger inside of her, pulling the dark lace fabric of her panties to one side, all the while kissing at her neck. "...how do I deserve a man like you?"

She traced her own hands down the muscles on his back, shivering with pleasure as he pulsed his fingers in and out of her.

"I am no man." He whispered the words against her throat, the sensation almost tickling her.

"But you are," she laughed in a whisper. "You're Eric. You're a man as I am a woman..."

"No..." He said the words firmer this time, almost growling them like some mad dog. He pulled his head up from her throat and then Claire froze upon seeing the face. It wasn't the face of Eric that she was looking at, it was his brother, Wraith.

"You?!" She tried to struggle free, but her arms and legs betrayed her, moving at a glacial pace, and with no strength at all. "Let me go!" she yelled. "Eric, Eric, save me!"

"He can't save you now," Wraith whispered with a frozen growl.

"Let me go, let me go!"

"I'll let you go. Just as soon as I've finished drinking you dry."

His lips snarled back, revealing the long-pointed lines of his fangs. He threw his mouth upon her neck, sinking the points into her flesh. Claire gasped when feeling the small punctures, which burned in her skin like fiery knives.

"No," she whispered, turning slowly, her whole body moving with no urgency, despite her will. "Please...stop." Her words became like molasses, her mind like ice. His fingers clutched her tighter, his grip holding her firm. His jaw pulsed against her throat, as he swallowed mouthfuls of her blood. He drank for what felt like a lifetime and when he let her go she fell, sinking into the leaf-covered ground, marveling at its softness.

"No..."

He stood over her, his red eyes glinting in the moonlight. He knelt down, and horror passed over her face, for it wasn't Wraith. It was Eric again.

"Yes," he smiled, laughing to himself darkly. "You're mine now, and I'll do with you as I wish. Whenever and whatever I like."

"No, no, no!"

*

Claire sat bolt upright in bed, her chest heaving in the darkness. Eric sprang awake next to her.

"What? What is it?!"

He turned the bedside lamp on, casting pale light across the dark room. Eric brushed a strand of hair from Claire's face. She was pale with fright, and her pupils were two fine points. As he brushed his fingers, color flushed in her cheeks, returning her face to its doll-like beauty.

"I don't know," Claire said honestly, unable to remember her dream. "Some nightmare I think. It was... I was in a forest, I think."

"It's okay." Eric placed an arm around her and they lay back on the bed again.

"I didn't even realize I'd fallen asleep." Claire turned to face Eric. She couldn't quite believe that she was really lying here with a man as beautiful as him. Just looking at him took her breath away.

"What are you thinking?" he asked, staring back into her eyes.

"Can't you just read my mind and know?"

"Well, yes. But you asked me not to. And I promised I wouldn't, so I won't."

Claire looked at Eric, warmth spreading across her chest. A smile crept across her face as she looked at him. Eric smiled too.

"What? What is it? What are you thinking?!"

"Nothing," she beamed. "You'll have to make do with not knowing."

"You're such a tease, Ms. Eldridge." His words whispered over her like soft silk. He placed a hand on the curve of her hip and squeezed his fingers into her flesh, pulling their bodies together.

She felt his hardness graze her stomach and bit her lip, wondering...

"Okay, I don't have to be a mind reader to tell you're thinking something naughty." Eric laughed. He moved his hand around the back of her and squeezed at her ass. Claire felt the urge to moan rising in her throat and fought against it.

"Come on," Eric whispered, shifting forward so their faces were closer. "What are you thinking?"

"I was just imagining what it would feel like to have your cock in my mouth." Claire dashed her gaze from his, looking down into the darkness of the sheets. She regretted saying it as soon as she had, and she felt her cheeks burning slightly in embarrassment.

"You don't just have to imagine," Eric said, clearing at something in his throat. "Why not find out for yourself?"

Claire's eyes darted back up to his. "You mean, you don't mind?"

Eric laughed. "Why on earth would I mind?"

"I was... well, I was just worried that you might not want me to. I know I'm not very attractive."

He placed a finger on her lips almost instantly.

"Never say that again." His voice flared like steel. It almost felt as if Eric was using his Intention, but Claire knew that it was just the conviction of his voice. "You're the most beautiful woman I've ever seen. I love every inch of your body from head to toe."

Claire felt a strange warmth bubbling up from within her chest, and she giggled. She'd never been complimented by a man like this before, and it felt strangely good.

"Okay." She smiled bashfully. She bit her lip once more and finally summoned the strength to glance at him quickly. She found herself excited for a moment, then another question rose in her mind, dashing her hopes.

"But... but what if I'm no good at it?"

"Well, I'm sure there's only one way to find out." Eric threw back the sheet with his hands, and wrapped his thumbs around the waistband of his boxer shorts. A moment later he was lying on his side before her, completely nude. His cock was fully erect, pre-cum dripping from the pink slit at the tip of his shaft, forming a small pool of damp on the mattress cover.

Claire flicked her eyes greedily over his body, taking every inch of his perfection in, not wanting to forget a moment of him. Just looking at Eric made her tingle between her legs. All she could imagine is how it would feel to be on top of him, sliding down slowly, moaning as his length cleaved her virgin walls in two.

"Can't we just..." She paused, thinking. "We should just...fuck me. *Please.*"

He crushed his body against hers, and she opened her mouth, surrendering to him completely. He had one arm around her back, and another around her hips, pulling her body against his. She moaned into his mouth, pressing her palms against the muscle of his chest. She was so wet, so open, so ready for him.

He pulled away. Breathing hard.

"I can't," he said. "Not yet. We have to wait until you're at peak arousal. You're not ready yet."

She opened her mouth to protest, but Eric placed a finger between her lips.

"You're not, trust me. This is just as hard for me as it is for you."

"Fine," Claire huffed, then a wry smile spread across her face.

She shifted her weight onto all fours, and positioned herself over his legs, so his crotch was directly below her head. She sat on his legs for a moment, staring down at his twitching mass.

"What are you doing?" Eric laughed.

Claire shifted her weight on his legs, pushing her swollen lips against the hard edge of his shins. She saw him swallow at something in his throat, and smiled at seeing she was having an effect on him.

"If you're going to tease me, then I'm going to tease you."

She pulled at the buttons on her pajama top slowly, unfastening them one by one from top to bottom. When she reached the bottom, she pulled at the bottom corners of the shirt, pulling the fabric taut against her large breasts, causing it to squeeze into her flesh ever so slightly.

Eric's cock twitched with hardness, lifting off his stomach for a moment.

"God, yes..." he moaned, hypnotized by her strip tease.

"Do you like this ...*Daddy?*" She whispered the question as lustfully as possible, surprising herself at how hot the words sounded coming from her mouth.

"Daddy likes it a lot," Eric said, flapping his mouth in shock.

She pulled the left half of her pajama shirt back from her breasts slowly, covering her nipple with her right hand. She eased her left arm out of the sleeve and then shifted hands quickly so her left hand was cupping her breast.

He twitched again and she looked down at him with a knowing smile. Claire had never done anything sexy like this for a man before, and knowing that she was having an effect on him was driving her wild.

"Keep going..." Eric pleaded. "Don't stop."

She pulled back the second side of the pajama shirt, repeating the striptease as she had done on the first half. When the top was completely removed, she threw it onto the floor and sat there for a moment, holding her breasts in her hands, twisting her wet crotch against his legs.

"You should come further up my body and do that on my dick," Eric suggested. "It would be much better for both of us."

"Maybe..." Claire whispered seductively, "But then how would I do this?"

She bent over slowly, placing her hands on the smooth muscle of his hips. She placed a solitary kiss at the point below his nipples and crawled back on the bed, working down his torso as she did so. It wasn't long until she reached the tip of his cock, which sprawled up his body in its gargantuan length, stopping midway between his belly button and his chest.

She licked the tip at first with the most delicate grace, brushing the very tip of her tongue against the head so lightly, like a faint whisper.

"Oh God!"

Claire smiled as she heard Eric gasp above her, his hands twitched from the bed to her hair, his fingers moving to sieve through her thick locks.

"Nah-ah." Claire lifted her hands from his hips, forcing his hands back to the mattress. "No hands. You're only allowed to watch."

He groaned in frustrated pleasure, twisting his hips from off the mattress, his cock lunging at her mouth. She opened her mouth and turned her head, sucking his shaft into her mouth and holding it there for a moment like a fleshy cob.

"Oh God, Claire, I don't know how much of this I can take."

She felt herself clenching at his words, her pussy positively dripping now. She twisted her hips against his thighs, pushing her wet panties against his legs.

"I want your cum in my mouth," she whispered.

Eric gasped in return. "Yes, fuck, yes."

She wrapped her slender hand around the mammoth girth of his shaft, groaning as she felt his warmth against her palm. She stroked her hand up and down his length slowly several times, relishing at how *solid* it felt in her grasp. Claire had often imagined—in her naughtier moments—what a cock would feel like in her hand. She stared in wonder at his dick as she moved her palm up and down the firm shaft, almost hypnotized by the motion herself.

"I can barely touch my fingers around you." She smiled, looking up at the torture on his face.

"You're so slow," he gasped, "so delicate. I can't bear it."

She felt his cock twitch under her hand several times over. She let go immediately, wagging her finger at him.

"Ah ah. No cumming just yet. Only in my mouth. Don't waste it."

He simply nodded, no words left to give. Claire almost felt surprised at the way she was acting. She had no idea where this... temptress was coming from. And she had no idea that she could have such an effect over a man, especially a man like Eric.

She took his cock in her hand again and pumped a few more times, a little quicker now. Pre-cum dripped from the pink slit at the tip of his bulbous head. She closed her eyes, relishing the feeling of his veins as her palm glided up and down, passing through her hand like thick ropes.

She paused to imagine what the ridges of his shaft would feel like pulsing against the walls of her cunt, and felt herself spasming a little at the thought. She let out a small but involuntary gasp of pleasure, causing Eric to look at her with a raised eyebrow.

"Just close your eyes and relax," she said, attempting to deflect attention from her.

She pumped at his shaft again, pulling it toward her and she lowered her mouth to the swollen tip of his cock. She wrapped her lips around it, pushing her tongue down to guide the firm tip into her mouth.

"Claire, fuck, fuck!" His whispered breath staggered into the dark as she slid her mouth down the shaft. She managed to work down half of his length before she found she could go no further.

I will get to the bottom at some point, she thought to herself, and she made a mental note to practice whenever she was alone.

For now it seemed that halfway was enough. She closed her eyes, humming in pleasure as she held his cock in her mouth, swirling her tongue around the thickness of his throbbing shaft. He continued to whisper words of encouragement and tortured pleasure.

Claire felt the mattress cover pulling away from her knees slightly. She didn't have to open her eyes to know that it was his hands, scrunching up the fabric in his palms. She lifted her head up quickly, pursing her lips around the very top of his cock.

She pushed her tongue into the slit, licking up the small drops of pre-cum. He tasted salty-sweet, an unusual but delicious taste that she longed to drink down deep.

"I can't last like this..." he moaned.

She kissed the tip of his cock, holding his base in her palm.

"Thirty more seconds," she purred softly, looking up at him. She took him in her mouth again, sliding down to the halfway point of his generous length once more, pulling back quicker this time, gliding her mouth into a fast but steady rhythm.

As her mouth bobbed up and down his length, she took her breast in her hand and palmed at it gently while gyrating her wetness against his legs.

A constant but steady trickle of moans escaped his mouth now, and it seemed that his cock was growing firmer with every pump of her mouth. She moved her head with swift firmness, rolling up and down the length, eyes closed, nostrils flaring, mouth humming.

"I can't..." he stammered, and she heard his arms moving and his fingers glancing through her hair. "I must...*please*."

She brought her lips to the top of his cock and whispered her permission.

"Cum."

The steel length of his cock twitched below instantly, and Claire wrapped her lips around the head to catch him. It came as a solitary burst at first, and then it came all at once. Thick, hot ropes of his cum, squirting up from the salty slit of his cock, pulsing into her mouth like molten fire, spouting onto her tongue and the roof of her mouth.

Her breath raced through her nose as she caught him, squeezing her hand tightly around his shaft as she focused all her concentration on drinking him up. His cock squeezed tight, flinching like rigid metal a dozen times over, fast first, but then slower, as each pulse of cum brought him nearer to the end of his climax.

She felt him soften in her mouth slightly, and when she was sure he was done, she sucked her lips up the head of his cock, keeping them pursed as he left her mouth, not wanting to spill a drop.

She sat up straight on his legs, swirling her tongue around her mouth, swallowing the remnants of his love down hungrily.

Eric lay on the bed, eyes closed, the back of his hand cast against his forehead. He opened his eyes and stared at the ceiling, and then he looked to her in bewilderment.

Claire noticed his chest was heaving up and down, and in noticing that she saw her own was too.

"That was... amazing..." Eric praised through rasping breaths.

Claire blushed, feeling silently proud of her accomplishment.

"You taste divine," she said, complimenting him back. "I would very much like to do that again."

"Oh... you are *very* welcome to," Eric laughed, and Claire lay down beside Eric, staring into his eyes. He looked at her like she was a prized treasure.

"Where did you learn to do that?" he asked. "I've never... it's never... you're amazing."

She giggled, feeling bashful at his words. "Was it really that good? I've never done it before. I was just moving through instinct I suppose."

"Well fuck me," Eric positively growled and slid his hand down the side of her body. "I can't wait to see how instinct works for the rest of you."

"Now?" she asked.

"No, but nice try."

Claire bit her lip in frustration.

"But when?"

"Soon, I promise. Besides... you're practically yawning. I'd be surprised if you could stay awake another minute."

"I'm fine..." Claire said in protest, but she could hear the tiredness in her voice. "But why? I don't know why I'm so sleepy."

"I told you. It takes a lot of energy to mate with a vampire. It's why I wanted to taste you first."

"But it was just my mouth..." she protested, her words meandering with fatigue.

"*Exactly*," Eric said, as if proving a point. "Imagine how much more energy it would take for full sex. We'll get there, I promise. The more pent up you get, the more you will be able to tolerate it."

"Okay..." Claire practically yawned the words, cuddling into the crook of his neck.

Eric pulled his arm tightly around her, shifting the covers back over them once more. She squeezed against the slow rhythm of his rising chest and her eyes closed, until slowly but surely, she fell asleep.

CHAPTER SIX

Eric

ERIC FELL INTO A DEEP AND DREAMLESS SLEEP just minutes after Claire, surprised that sleep was so effortless to him when she was in his arms. He had always struggled with rest, haunted by visions of his past which kept him up for hours on end.

They both lay there sleeping in silenced comfort for hours, until the sun sank beneath the mountains, casting long dark shadows across the valley beneath the castle.

A knock came at the door several hours after, causing them both to wake in a confused stir.

Eric swung his legs from out of the bed at the sound of the timid knock.

"Eric?"

He turned at Claire's confused whispers as she stirred. "Who is it?"

"It's okay, darling." He brushed hair from her rosy face.

She sat up in the bed, pulling the quilt tightly around her, a trace of fear glinting in her eyes as she stared at the door across the room.

"But what if..."

"It's not him," he said, putting the notion to bed. "He won't come up here ever again, not after what happened in the library."

Claire swallowed and nodded silently, seeming to believe his words.

The timid knock came once more, pulling Eric's attention from the girl.

"All right, all right!" He rose from the bed with haste and grabbed a charcoal robe, wrapping the plush fabric around him.

He reached the door in a dozen silent steps, and paused for a moment as his hand hovered over the handle, listening to the guest on the other side.

Sophia... he thought as he felt the presence of his youngest sister. He turned the handle, pulling the door ajar ever so slightly.

"Eric! Hi!" The saccharine tone of her timid voice floated into the room.

Eric relaxed seeing that it was only Sophia, and no one else. Veronica would have been a headache to deal with at this time of night. Sophia had always been his favorite sibling, and the one that he felt closest to.

Still, she was disturbing his time with Claire, and he felt slightly uncomfortable at her being here.

"Sophia... can I help you?"

The young raven-haired girl seemed to bounce on her heels almost. To the outside perspective, she would have seemed almost still, but Eric could read the faintest trace of her body language like a book. Although she appeared to be standing almost perfectly still, he saw her more as bouncing off the walls in excitement.

"Is it true?" Her eyes sparked with wonder. Sophia tilted her head slightly, trying to glimpse within his room.

Eric held the door firmly, pushing his body up against the gap to remove any chance of her seeing inside.

"Is what true?" Eric said, trying to play dumb.

"Come on, brother!" Sophia dropped all hopes of containing her excitement and her whole body slumped momentarily as she said the words with dreary impatience. "Wraith has told Father. You must have come to expect that by now!"

Eric pushed the tongue against the inside of his cheek and rolled his eyes. He didn't answer, but the considerable sigh from his body was answer enough that he knew what she was talking about.

"The library." Sophia's eyes bulged. "He said you nearly killed him!"

"As I have at least once a month for the last hundred years."

"But for *real* this time, Eric. I was in Father's room when he came in. He was *shaking.*"

"Good." Eric smiled, finding pleasure at the thought of his brother in terror.

"He said you have a *girl.*"

"So?" Eric passed it off as nothing. "I have girls in here all the time. What's new?"

"No you don't. Not for several years at least. He said you're up to something, he said she was *different...*"

Eric steeled his jaw at the comment. He hadn't supposed that Wraith had noticed the peculiar rarity that was the power held inside Claire.

"Is it true? Can I meet her? Is she nice?"

Eric felt like sighing again.

He had wanted to keep Claire secret to protect her. There was no safer place to keep her but the castle, and at the same time nowhere more dangerous.

He knew that his family would find out eventually, but he hadn't anticipated it being this soon. He wanted to turn Claire before he presented her to his family. That way it would eliminate the chance of anyone else doing it before he could.

"Fine." He gave up the pretense of lying, knowing that Sophia was too smart to fall for it anyway.

"It is true, but please, I want you to keep this quiet."

Eric had to play his cards right. Sophia was no immediate threat to him. Vampires may have been slightly different in their reproductive qualities, but there was no way that Sophia could impregnate Claire, no matter how fertile Claire may be.

There was the chance that Sophia could turn her, claiming her for herself. But without claiming her womb as human first, it would negate all the breeding potential of her body. She'd be a vampire, but she'd be just like the rest, unable to reproduce.

Should I tell her?

He weighed the question in his mind. There every chance that Sophia would see Claire for what she really was anyway—a breeder. If Eric told his sister first, it would make him appear more trusting of her—which he was.

"Give us a moment to dress." Eric said tersely.

"You promise you won't escape from the window?!" Sophia bounced on her heels once more, trying to see inside the room.

Eric laughed.

"Relax, sister. You're being paranoid."

He closed the door and considered her idea for a moment, before pushing it to the back of his mind. Eric didn't want to risk Claire getting cold. He didn't want to hurt her like that ever again.

"Who is it?" Claire said, sitting up in the bed with the covers clutched at her chest.

"It's my sister," Eric said as he walked to the wardrobe. He slipped his gown from his body, placed it back on a hanger, and grabbed his clothes from the dresser.

"Sister?" Claire said the word with a tense wariness. "But... what does she want?"

"It's all right," Eric said as he pulled his clothes on. "Dress. She wants to meet you. She's not like Wraith. She's nice. Nicer than I am."

"Meet *me*? Why?" Claire slid out of bed, dressing herself in pajamas as she had nothing else to wear.

"She's just curious," Eric said. "She's lovely, honestly. The nicest vampire you'll ever meet."

Eric half said the words to placate Claire, but there was only truth in them. He often thought of the Castle Belmont and its inhabitants as a black rose bush, lying in the shadow with its hundreds of thorns turned in on itself. The thorns where the many characters who roamed its hallways, yet in the middle of the dark and twisted thorns there was a small light, and that light was Sophia.

Sophia was younger than Eric, and the youngest of all their siblings in fact. There had always been a perceptible innocence about her that made all those close to her feel as though they had the urge to protect her. She was dainty, frail-looking, and her personality was jubilant and sparkling—like a bauble bouncing on a tree branch, catching light and scattering it across the room in all directions.

For the longest time, Sophia had mirrored Eric in his own darkness, but she had always taken to it with firm reluctance. It was her own almost inward revulsion at what she was that contributed to Eric looking at himself and realizing that being a vampire didn't have to mean being a murderer. They still had to drink blood of course—they always did—but there was a humane way of doing it and being alive.

"Nicest vampire?" Claire seemed to almost laugh, and Eric breathed with relief seeing she was a little calmer. He fetched a robe for her from the wardrobe and wrapped it around her shoulders.

"Yes. Honestly. She's lovely, she's a darling. You have nothing to fear. I think you'll get on rather well, actually."

"Okay." Her eyes darted around the room in nervousness.

"And I'll get you some clothes," he said, looking down at her pajamas and robe. "I apologize for being such a bad host."

"That's all right." Claire leaned in and kissed his cheek, gliding her hand up the inside of his thigh, just glancing the fullness of his cock. "I don't intend on wearing clothes all that much when you're around anyway."

Eric fought the urge to groan and turned from Claire, biting his lip to keep himself from jumping on her.

"Come." He tilted his head for her to walk to the door. Eric pulled it open fully this time, although still with apprehension, and Sophia set her eyes upon Claire for the first time.

"Oh you *are* just lovely." Sophia shook her head in wonder, stepping into Eric's room, ignoring him completely. "I'm Sophia," she said, her timid voice ringing through the room like a glass bell.

Sophia held her hand out and Claire took it, shaking it out of politeness. Sophia held her hand for a moment, and Eric knew that she was listening to the pulse within her hand.

"There's no reason to be so nervous," Sophia said, releasing Claire's hand. "I'm not like Wraith at all."

"How did you...?" Claire began to ask how she'd known what she was thinking, then she realized. "Oh."

"Oh yes," Sophia beamed, looking from Claire to Eric. "Telepathy. A gift that we are blessed with, and you will find that you are blessed with it too when Eric comes to turn you."

"Sophia!" Eric practically hissed the words, but it sounded more like strained disappointment. He flared his real thoughts into Sophia's mind.

I haven't spoken with her about turning yet!

Cold realization spread over Sophia's face at her mistake.

"I'm sorry, Eric." She swallowed. "I didn't mean to..."

"What does she mean, Eric?" Claire said, turning her head at him, confused. "You're going to *turn* me? Make me vampire?" Claire's voice seem to flare, annoyance rising in it.

"No Claire, you don't understand—"

"Is that before or after you put a child in my belly? Or do I not get a say in that matter either?"

86

Eric winced at her words, closing his eyes, for now Sophia knew the full truth too.

He lifted his eyes with slow reluctance to meet his sister's gaze. She was staring at him, mouth open just as he expected, her gaze flitting from him to Claire and back again.

"She? You? No..." The shock seemed to affect Sophia's ability to speak, and she stammered as her eyes almost bulged from her head.

She looked back to Claire again. "You're a breeder!"

Eric flew across the room in a glance, shutting the door and locking it, and then sweeping across once more so he was but an inch from Sophia's mouth. He held his finger against her lips, urging her to be deathly quiet.

To Eric and Sophia, he had moved with a quickness, but a quickness that was nothing out of the ordinary.

Claire, however, stood almost in shock, as she watched the ribbon that was Eric, blurring through the apartment in rapid motion.

"You have to be quiet, Sophia," Eric said with whispering urgency.

"But, but... she's a breeder! It's true!" Sophia said it out loud again, the shock overriding her brain.

"Okay, okay!" Eric clamored. "Now you know our secret, but please stop saying it out loud. Don't say it, don't think it, don't *feel* it! Heavens knows, Father has probably felt your reaction already!"

Eric knew that his father could seek out the thoughts of most inhabitants of the castle at any time—such was the strength of his long and latent power. It was highly unlikely that he would be making much effort to follow Sophia, but the chance was there, and Eric didn't want to risk his father finding out before he could tell him.

"But this is wonderful!" Sophia gasped, beaming from Eric to Claire. "Oh, you're such a beauty Claire, and I can already tell that we're going to be the best of friends."

Sophia's raw enthusiasm seemed to disarm any of the wayward annoyance that Claire was holding, ready to project to Eric when they had a moment alone.

"Why, thank you, Sophia," Claire said, abashed. "You're very pretty too. I hope we can be good friends."

Eric was momentarily relieved that Claire seemed to sense that Sophia wasn't a threat. There was still the issue at hand of the whole castle being aware of his secret.

"Listen to me, Sophia." Eric clutched his sister by the shoulders. Her attention was fixed firmly in amazement on Claire. He turned her face to his, speaking into her eyes.

"I know this is amazing for you, and I know that you've never met a breeder before, but we have to keep this secret. We have to keep this between us."

"But Eric—"

She attempted to speak, but Eric put a finger to his lips.

"Just hear me out. She *is* a breeder. It's true, okay? I've admitted it to you now, but you have to understand that we have to be very delicate about how we deliver this information to the castle. There are a lot of vampires out there who would seek to take Claire from me if they knew I hadn't claimed her yet."

"But Eric—"

He pushed his finger against her lips again.

"Please. That's why we have to keep it quiet, okay? And you need to promise me that you won't tell anyone. Not Father, not Veronica, not Ira, and especially not Wraith."

Eric knew there was no danger of Sophia telling Wraith. Although they were technically brother and sister they couldn't be more different. Sophia had little regard for Wraith, and spent as much time away from him as possible.

Sophia twisted Eric's hand from her face and stepped back, clutching it in her grasp.

"But Eric, that's what I've been trying to tell you this whole time! That's what I've been trying to say! Why do you think I'm here in the first place?"

"What are you talking about?" he said, his eyes searching into hers with manic despair.

"Wraith already *knows*. He figured it out back in the library. That's why he was so desperate to get to Father. He wanted to be the first to let him know!"

Eric pulled his hand from hers, almost feeling as if all the strength in his body had drained to the floor. He stumbled back from her, feeling stunned.

"Father knows?"

"Yes, Eric, that's what I came here to tell you. Veronica wanted to come, but I told her not to. I said that you seeing her here would only annoy you, and it would be best if I came."

"But you... you acted as if you didn't know just now?"

"I didn't believe it myself until I heard the words come from your mouth."

Eric nodded slightly at her words, agreeing with them. He got on with Veronica in a faint capacity. She wasn't as bad as Wraith, but she wasn't as angelic as Sophia either. He knew that she would find the gossip wickedly fun, and he could just imagine how she would gloat as she delivered the news to him.

"But what did he say?" Eric said, his eyes flying up to meet Sophia. "What did Father say?!"

A corner of her mouth pulled to one side and she half-shrugged. "He didn't say much, really. You know what he's like with his words. He keeps everything under lock and key."

Eric dropped his head. "But he must have said something. He must have given you some indication of how he felt."

Now that his father knew, the whole castle would know, and that wasn't good for Eric. They would start coming for her. He'd have to take her fast, but he didn't want to risk moving too quickly and forcing Claire when her body wasn't ready.

"Well, he wants to meet her, naturally."

Eric looked up at his sister in shock.

"What?"

"Why else would I come up here? Other than to meet the lovely Claire of course." She nodded at Claire, who smiled back politely. "He sent me up here," Sophia continued. "Father sent me up here with an invitation for you to bring Claire to meet him."

Eric sank to the bed, and what little color existed in his pale cheeks drained almost completely.

Claire, sensing that there was something about the news that was dreadfully frightening to Eric, sat beside him on the bed, brushing her palm down his back.

"It's all right," Claire said. "It's probably a little sooner for meeting your parents than I would have liked," she joked, attempting to lighten the mood. "I'll do my best to be charming, however."

"You don't understand, Claire," Eric said, shaking his head in dread like a man who had been condemned to die. "It's not my father that I'm worried about. It's the castle. Now they know that you're here, every male vampire under this spired roof will be vying to claim you before I can."

"But that's ridiculous!" Claire scoffed. "I won't let them do that."

"It's not a case of letting them..."

"Oh, Eric, you're right," Sophia said, finally catching on to why he'd wanted so much secrecy in the first place. "You don't think this will bring back the bad people do you?"

"Bring them back?" Eric rose from the bed and walked to the window, pulling up the dark blind, revealing the vast and swollen midnight vista of the valley floor below. He turned back to Sophia and Claire, his face etched with a grave expression. "They never left. They've been hiding here, waiting, all this time. We can trust no one now, Sophia. Tonight we will learn who our real friends are."

Eric looked at Claire. "Claire. Get ready."

"Where are we going?"

"We're going to visit my father."

By Zara Novak

CHAPTER SEVEN

Claire

THEY WERE ON THE WAY TO VISIT ERIC'S father when the first one attacked. After walking down several flights of stairs and through a long stone tunnel that cut through the mountain, they emerged on the western wing of Castle Belmont.

"Stay very still," Eric said as they walked around a corner. "Something is hunting us."

Claire swallowed at something in her throat, taking a step back from Eric. He stood perfectly still, staring at the empty stone corridor ahead. Next thing Claire knew, the corridor was a blast of noise and sound. A strange and ghastly voice filled the air amid the chaos.

"Give it to us!"

Claire pulled into a corner, and threw her hands over her head.

"You crossed the wrong Belmont today."

Claire opened her eyes at the sound of Eric's voice, and she saw him standing over a tall and gaunt-looking vampire. He was holding the vampire off the ground by his shirt, a stake pressed against his chest.

"You can't kill me. I'm your father's oldest ally!"

"You should have thought of that before you sought to claim my mate."

The gaunt vampire snarled his teeth. His dark gray eyes rolled around in his wicked head, flicking back and forth from Claire to Eric.

"You shouldn't be walking through here with a breeder!" his voice hissed, sounding like metal on dry stone. "You're asking for trouble!"

Claire could see Eric was debating whether or not to respond, but he didn't. He simply pushed the stake into the vampire's chest, causing the creature to let out a tortured scraping sound that somewhat resembled a scream.

The creature burst into a cloud of dust and ash. Eric stood up, looking back to Claire.

"Are you—"

"Eric, behind you!"

Eric turned to heed Claire's warning, but not fast enough. Another creature had pounced down the length of the corridor. In one swift move it grabbed Eric and launched him against the stone wall. Eric's body crumpled through the wall like a wrecking ball, knocking a huge hole in the side of the corridor and into the room next door.

The attacker looked in the direction it had thrown Eric and let out a single deep laugh from its barreled chest.

"Vampires." The creature shook his head then settled his eyes on Claire. "So fucking weak."

The thing confidently strode toward Claire, while she remained frozen in the corner. Claire looked upon the creature with horror. Not a vampire, not a man, some sort of moving statue.

"Come here, pretty darling," the creature's deep voice boomed from its mammoth body. It reached out to grab Claire, and its stone hand was nearly upon her when Eric jumped back into the corridor.

"Stop right there, golem. You have no need for a woman. What are you doing?"

The creature stopped and turned to face Eric. "I may not, but there are many vampires who would pay a good price for her. Stay away, vampire, your strength cannot match my own."

"I'll kill you before I let you touch her."

The stone giant laughed. "Just try. We both know vampires can't hurt golems."

Claire's eyes flicked from the golem to Eric and back again. Eric looked like a coiled spring, ready to strike. He didn't have a chance to attack the creature though, for the next thing bright red fire burst through the corridor, hitting the stone creature squarely in the chest.

The golem burst into a cloud of rock and dust. Claire turned from the explosion, but she was still covered from head to toe in dust. Eric was back beside her in a blur, standing in front of her and the source of the red fire. Claire looked around and saw a young woman, with ebony skin and black curly hair. She wore a long opal dress that matched the color of her eyes.

"Ezra?!" Surprise marred Eric's voice. "I thought you were fighting the White Order... what on earth are you doing here?!"

"I'm back." The ebony skinned woman stepped toward them, her crystal-blue eyes looking Claire up and down. "You must be Claire." She held out a hand and Claire took it. "I'm Ezra. Resident witch of the Castle Belmont." She turned back to look at Eric. "Looks like I got back just in the nick of time. What did I miss?"

Eric eyed her, still looking as if he was in disbelief.

"Don't fear, Eric. I know breeders are a rarity in your kind, but I'm not here to fight you. My allegiance lies with Castle Belmont, as it always has."

Eric seemed to relax a little at her words.

"How did you know she was a breeder?"

"I saw this several moons ago. It was a rare possibility, but it seems it *has* come to fruition."

"You knew this would happen and you didn't tell me?"

"You know that I cannot share that information with you. I don't think I could even if I wanted to."

Eric nodded.

"But what are you doing back? I thought you were fighting with the York Clan?"

"I was, but there has been a major setback. The White Order are winning the fight. One of their generals has grown strong. Too strong."

"Black magic?"

"There's not a doubt in my mind."

Eric's eyes widened at the news.

"I came back to ask your father for assistance. Will and Eli are coming too. They are a day behind my position."

"This is not good," Eric said, shaking his head.

Ezra's eyes were back on Claire again.

"You need to claim her fast, Eric. This whole castle will eat itself alive trying to get her."

"I know. Thank you, Ezra. Thanks for handling the golem."

"Anytime, Eric. Stay safe."

Claire stared in disbelief as the woman wisped through the wall in a cloud of blue smoke.

"Come." Eric grabbed Claire by the hand and pulled her down the corridor. "Before anyone else tries to attack."

*

They made it to Eric's father without any further altercations. Upon entering the room Claire saw the fair-haired vampire sitting at a desk, writing. At seeing them enter, he rose and attended to them both immediately. He looked older than Eric, but no older than forty at the most. There was a similarity between Eric and his father, but mostly he took after his mother. Atticus had long fair hair, which he kept groomed back neatly.

He looked tired, but well kept. He had the same rugged handsomeness as Eric. His face was softer in general, and the corner of his eyes were marred with the faint impression of crows feet. His lips were thin and white, his nose long and straight. The eyes were the thing that he and Eric had in common. They were smart and sharp, calculating like a cat on the hunt.

"Son."

The gentleman met his son with a soft smile, setting a hand on his shoulder.

"Father. This is Claire. Claire, this is Atticus Belmont. My father and leader of the Belmont family."

Atticus took his hand from Eric's shoulder and twined his fingers around Claire's. He pulled her hand to his mouth and kissed it softly.

"Claire it is an absolute pleasure to make your acquaintance."

"And yours too, sir." Claire's voice sounded timid, compared to the smooth velvet of Atticus's voice.

He let her hand go and turned his attention back to Eric.

"I trust your trip here wasn't too fraught?"

Eric rolled his eyes, his composure seeming to tighten a little. "You know what the trip here was like. Now the word is out, every man and his dog wants to take Claire."

"Who made the first move?"

"Nash. Rasputin Nash. He attacked us on the west corridor at the eave of the mountain pass."

Atticus's eyebrows lifted a little.

"Nash? The old dog. Didn't think he'd have it in him."

"He's dust now."

Atticus nodded at Eric's statement, as if it were the only logical response.

"You're not mad?" Eric said. "He's been an ally of ours for two centuries."

"Yes," Atticus said. "And look how fast he turned at news of there being a breeder here. Good riddance."

"It will put a strain on our relationship with the Nash vampires who remain at Castle Belmont."

"Maybe, as it will with all vampires who seek to take what's ours. This isn't the first time our allies have turned on us, and it won't be the last. Who else attacked?"

"A Golem. I think his name was Gendrir."

"Gendrir." Atticus nodded his head, indicating he was familiar with the creature. "He's a guardian for the Templemont family."

"Was," Eric corrected his father. Atticus raised his eyebrows in surprise once more.

"You killed him?"

"No." Eric shook his head. "Ezra. Lucky for me she's returned early."

"Ah. Yes. I will be meeting with her shortly after you leave. And it brings me to the reason I asked you here. Come, sit. Both of you."

Atticus walked across his study, taking a seat in a chair by the fire. Eric took Claire's hand, and led her across the room to two seats which sat opposite from Atticus.

"So you didn't just bring me here to risk Claire's life?"

Atticus scoffed. "Come on, son, you know me better than that. The castle would have found out eventually. It was important that you put on a show of strength to dissuade rebellion. By walking Claire through the castle, you've weeded out the first of your opponents. You know which families stand against you now."

"It's clever, I'll admit. But it risked Claire's life. Couldn't you have come to visit me?"

Atticus simply smiled, shaking his head.

"You have a breeder now. Get used to defending her with your life, until you turn her, anyway. It was the same when I found your mother. You have to demonstrate to the castle that you're not afraid to walk the hallways of your home. If the vampires here get the sense you're afraid, they'll turn on you."

Eric nodded at his father's sage advice. Claire saw the sense in it, even if the trip had scared her half to death.

"So what of the other business? Why did you summon me?"

"As you bumped into Ezra, I'm sure you may already know, but the York Clan are having trouble with the White Order. I sent Ezra to assist them with their fight, but things are not going as well as they hoped. William and Eli York will be joining me here tomorrow to present their case."

"What do they want?"

"More bodies. I'm asking that you and Wraith go with them."

Claire flinched at Wraith's name, and both Eric and Atticus noticed the gesture. Atticus looked at Claire.

"You have no cause to fear my son. I know he has wronged you, but he will not wrong you again. I have told him what the consequence of any further meddling will bring."

Claire stared at Atticus, frozen in suspense at his words.

"I will kill him myself."

Claire gasped. "You'd kill your own son?"

"Only if he disobeyed me. Which he will not. I'm no seer, but you don't have to be a witch to see that you and Eric are made for each other. Your bond wouldn't work with anyone else."

Even Eric seemed surprised at his father's words.

"Father, what on earth do you mean?"

"Something that a lot of people don't know about breeders is that they are only aligned with a select type of vampire. I can see it just looking at the two of you. The same connection that I once shared with your mother."

The men both fell silent, and Claire felt a weight fall in the room. Whatever had happened with Eric's mother, it seemed to be a sore spot for both him and his father.

Eric let out a sigh, then returned to the topic at hand.

"I can't assist with the York clan," he said, shaking his head. "I won't help a family who were so recently our enemy. I can't leave Claire here on her own."

"You can, and you will. I'm sorry, Eric, but this isn't up for debate. The Yorks may once have been our enemies, but we are united now, and we must stand united if we hope to defend ourselves from the White Order."

Claire looked at Eric, whose fists were clenched tight around the arms of the chair he was sitting on.

"Relax, son. Your assistance is not needed immediately, but you *will* help when it is required. There is plenty of time for you to carry out your plans with Claire."

"Very well," Eric answered tersely.

"So?" his father said. "Is it settled? William and Eli will be here tomorrow. Can I count on you to help?"

Eric thought for a moment and stood to his feet.

"I will help, but Claire comes first. Always."

"Understandable, son." Atticus rose to his feet too, and Claire followed.

The father and son looked at each other for a moment, mutual respect passing between them. Atticus turned his attention on Claire once more, his warm eyes sparkling at the sight of her.

"You are a true beauty, Claire, and my son is lucky to have you. I wish you both the best in your endeavors."

"Thank you, sir." Claire found she was touched by the vampire's kind words.

"And Eric."

"Hmm?" Eric looked from the fire to his father.

"Treat her well. Make sure you bond soon. I don't need to mention this, but this more than secures your inheritance of my throne. Be wary. Your true friends and enemies will reveal themselves over the coming days."

"Thank you, Father."

"No bother, son. Now go, both of you. I have a meeting with a witch that I must attend."

*

Eric quickly guided Claire back through the castle, his hand held firmly around hers all the while. As they walked Claire made small talk. She could sense that Eric was tense; she could sense that there would be some impending attack. She talked to attempt to distract herself, to distract him.

"He was nice," she said as Eric led them down the stone tunnel that bisected the mountain. "Your father..."

"He is," Eric said. "And that is how he got his power. A lot of people make the mistake of underestimating him. Atticus Belmont always gets what he wants."

As they walked through the labyrinth of stone, tapestry, and torch light, Claire attempted to make some effort of memorizing their passage. She was deep in the process of tracking their last six turns when Eric froze. Claire looked up and saw a vampire clutching a leather doctor's bag, standing at the opposite end of the corridor. He was deadly still for a moment, before turning his head and speaking.

"Ira. What are you doing here?"

Ira looked up from a journal that was in his hands. Claire noticed the peculiarity of the man's dress. While the other vampires she had seen in the castle dressed in a fairly contemporary manner, the vampire Eric had called Ira looked like a Victorian professor.

"Eric!" Ira looked up in surprise, barely seeming to notice that Eric and Claire had been there at all. He closed the leather tome in his hands and tucked it under his arm. He walked toward Claire and Eric with a broad smile on his face.

"You must be the lovely Claire." Ira smiled at Claire warmly, then looked at Eric. "I understand why you were in such haste back in the blood room the other day."

Eric's body seemed to relax. "Ira. You're not... not going to attack?"

"Heavens no!" The tweed-clad doctor rocked back on his heels, letting out a sharp laugh. "I have no interest in developing an heir, as useful as that may be. My real passion lies in knowledge, boy, you know that. Involving myself in... all this nonsense, it would take up too much of my time."

"But what are you doing here?" Eric said.

"I've been summoned to visit Juniper Nash. She wants me to read the last rights for Rasputin."

"Ah." Eric nodded solemnly at the mention of the vampire he had just dispatched.

Ira stepped around Claire and Eric, walking down the corridor behind them. "Lovely to meet you, Claire. We shall have to talk at further length when the time is more appropriate!"

The spindle-limbed doctor waved before turning a corner, disappearing into the recess of the castle. Claire looked at Eric in confusion, attempting to gather some sort of explanation.

Eric closed his eyes and shook his head from side to side. "I'll explain at some point, I promise. Let's just get back to the room for now. I'm tired and I need to rest."

*

As soon as they were back to the room, Claire practically jumped on Eric. He welcomed her touch, his lips pushing back against her eagerly. He brought his hands around the curves of her waist, pulling her body against his.

"You're certainly full of energy," Eric said, looking at Claire with his eyes sparkling. "What's gotten into you?"

She sunk her teeth into her lip, contemplating his question.

"You. Watching you defend me like that, out in the castle, it was..."

"Scary?"

"Fucking hot."

Eric let out a laugh at her admission. Claire had been bashful when she first arrived, feeling like a silly schoolgirl whenever she admitted the effect he had on her. She didn't care anymore though. She wanted him to know.

She looked up at Eric, the want for him easily visible in her eyes. Upon seeing her lust, the smile quickly fell from Eric's face.

"How long do I have to wait until I get what I want?" Claire closed the distance between Eric and herself, pushing her crotch against his through the fabric of their clothes. Eric swallowed at something in his throat. He squeezed his hands at the flesh of her ass, crushing her body against his.

"And what is it you want?" he said, drawing his lips down her neck.

Claire let out a gasp of pleasure at the hotness of his breath.

"I want you down there. You won't fuck my... my *pussy* yet." She practically whispered the word, which felt so dirty to her. "So please. I'm begging you. Take me in the other place, until we can have sex. I need to feel you inside of me."

She felt something stir in his trousers, pressing against her stomach like a hot iron. Eric took Claire by the hand and pulled her into the bathroom.

"Come," he said quickly, shutting the door behind them. He turned the jets on in the tub, filling the tiled basin with hot water.

"What are you doing?" Claire giggled as Eric practically tore the clothes from her body.

"Bathing with you the other day is probably one of the hottest things I've ever done."

Claire almost felt herself blushing at his comment. He moved around her, undressing her with a surprising swiftness. His lips kissed her body as he unclasped her bra. His fingertips brushed over her skin as he tucked his thumbs into her panties and rolled them down her thighs.

Before Claire knew it, he was naked too. They stood naked against one another as the jets ran, kissing passionately.

"Look." Eric turned Claire around and stood with her in the mirror. Claire covered herself instantly at the sight of her body. Next to Eric she was unsightly.

"Stop that." He grabbed her hands and stopped her from covering herself.

"But I'm so *round*," Claire protested. "I look like a sack of dough compared to you. You're a living Adonis."

Eric stepped to the side so he was standing in front of her. He pressed a finger against her lips, while his other hand smoothed over her buttocks.

"What did I tell you about criticizing yourself? If you carry on disobeying me, I might have to punish you..."

Claire laughed as Eric sank to his knees. He left a trail of kisses down her body as he did so. She was about to come back with a snarky response when she felt his mouth pressing against her cunt.

"Well I...ah!"

The pleasure took Claire by surprise, and her whole body lurched in response. She threaded her fingers through his dark hair, holding him against her as his tongue pushed between her wet folds.

"Oh Eric..." Claire moaned, running a hand up her body to squeeze her breast. "Please fuck me. I need you inside me so bad." She clenched hard with her need for him. He pulled away for a moment and pushed the tip of his tongue against her wet line, licking upward slowly. The delicacy of the movement made her feel desperate with lust.

"Eric, yes, Eric!"

He thrust his tongue inside of her, affectionately lapping between her folds. The sensation was too much for her to bear. Her hips bucked against him, her cunt aching to be pressed harder against his warm and soft mouth. He slipped a hand between her legs from behind, stroking a finger down her ass. He slipped between her cheeks and rubbed the finger against the tight hole, drawing small circles with the pad of his finger.

She found pleasure in the sensation and dropped her head back. With one hand clutched on his head, and the other on her breast, Claire looked up to the ceiling and closed her eyes as she moaned.

"Fuck, yes!"

His tongue flicked wildly across her bud, causing the warmth inside her to multiply until she could bear it no longer. He moved his finger from her ass to her pussy, brushing it up and down the line of her cunt, gathering her juices on his digit. He moved it back to her ass and pushed up, applying pressure to her hole.

Claire's hips bucked at the dual sensation of his tongue on her clit, and his finger on her ass. She steeled her heels against the tile floor, feeling the urge to lower herself down onto him. She felt him push against her hole, and his finger slipped inside of her, all the way up to his knuckle. She gasped at the sensation, finding it utterly divine. She clenched around him, rocking her hips back and forth. Her fingers scrunched through his hair, his tongue lapped up and down against the line of her cunt.

She came, and she came hard.

"Yes, fuck, yes, yes, yes!"

Her eyes scrunched tight as fire exploded across her body, emanating from her core and arcing out in every direction until it filled her completely. She felt herself clenching around his finger, finding even more pleasure in the sensation of being filled there. Her fingers kept him held firmly against her, but she knew even if they weren't there, he'd stay, lapping at her lovingly until he knew she was done.

She felt lips on her own, and she opened her eyes to see Eric was kissing her. He had stood up now and had his arms around her again.

"How was that, my darling?" He kissed her forehead. She breathed slowly and she breathed deep, the scent of her juice on his lips and in the air.

"I don't know how you do that to me," she replied hazily. She felt lust-drunk, stupefied by the presence of his affection.

"Come." He grabbed her by the hand and led her into the tub, which was now full. He turned off the jets and they lowered themselves into the steaming water slowly.

Claire let out a loud sigh of satisfaction as she melted into the contours of the tiled tub. Eric sat across from her with his arms outspread on the rim. He smiled at her knowingly, and straightened his legs so his big toe was grazing her pussy under the water.

After a minute or two Claire finally recovered the ability to speak and think.

"How do you do that?" she said once more, able to think clearly now.

"What?" Eric smirked. "Eat your pussy?"

"Not just that." Claire blinked hard. "Everything. All of it. You're so good. It feels so good every time. I never want to stop."

"That brings comfort to me," he said. "But we're only getting started. It's important that I get you worked up as much as possible, for when we finally fuck. Until then..."

She felt his hands wrap around her legs and pull her across the tub toward him. She opened her legs so she was straddling him. Her pussy pushed against his crotch and she felt that he was hard again. She wanted nothing more than to lift herself up and slowly sink down his shaft, until he bottomed out and filled her completely.

Eric brought his mouth to her nipples and sucked at them, worshiping her breasts with his mouth. Claire let out a gasp of pleasure and her hips bucked involuntarily against his cock. They ground against each other under the water, his hands held firmly around her waist.

"Please," she moaned between him sucking her nipples. "Please, I need you inside me."

She felt his cock tense at her words.

"I want to be inside of you, darling. But you know the rules. Let us wash. Then we'll go to bed."

They spent another fifteen minutes in the bath like that, Eric lavishing her with affection, which felt more like torture every minute he wasn't pushing his cock inside of her. He washed her, and Claire washed him in turn. He moved with deliberate slowness, lathering up every inch of her body, taking extra time with her breasts and her ass.

When it was her turn to wash him, she wanted to rush. She wanted nothing more than to get to the bedroom with him, but she found she wanted to take her time. Drawing her soaped-up hands over his hard muscles was too exciting to hurry.

By the time they were both done, he took her by the hand and pulled her from the bath. Then they dried each other off, which was really just another excuse for him to place his hands on her body again.

Eric picked Claire up in his arms, and she found herself surprised at his strength, despite him having picked her up before. She wrapped her legs around him and they kissed as he walked her into the bedroom.

Apart from the light in the bathroom, the rest of the room was dark. Eric slowly set Claire down onto the bed, kissing her on the forehead.

"I'll be right back."

"Where are you going?" She eyed the outline of his erection in the dimness.

"You want to play, don't you? I need to get my toys."

She bit her lip in anticipation, a wry smile spreading across her face.

"Okay."

Eric walked back into the bathroom and she was left alone in the dark on the bed. Claire decided she would have some fun, and make herself ready for him upon his return. She turned around so she was on all fours, spreading her knees so he would have a good vantage of her ass and pussy.

She'd never done anything like this before. She'd never been so open with a man. Before Eric, Claire didn't think she'd ever have the ability to be so brash with a man, but there was something about him that just brought this out in her. She placed her weight onto her elbows and lowered her face down until it was on the mattress. The cover of the bed grazed her nipples slightly, and she found it nice.

She clenched at the thought of him returning, and heard her wetness in the dark room.

"I've got a few for us to begi—"

She heard him stop, and smiled to herself, imagining his face upon seeing her.

"Good Lord." His feet padded across the carpet quietly, and she felt his knees sinking onto the bed. He smoothed his hands over her ass, exploring her hole and her pussy freely now. "What have I done to deserve you?"

"Fuck me, Eric," she whispered through tortured breaths. "Fuck me. I want you inside of me."

He said nothing in return. All she heard was the clicking of a cap, a bottle maybe.

"What are you doing?"

"Lube," he said. "Here."

Cold wetness dripped onto her, starting from the top of her ass. He squeezed a generous amount onto her, then he set the bottle down and rubbed the cool gel across her ass.

"Oh fuck!" Claire's hands gathered up small mountains of fabric in her palms while Eric massaged the lubricant over her skin. With one hand he pushed his thumb into her hole, submerging it gently. With his other hand he held two fingers out, brushing them up and down her wide pussy. He slipped them in, pulled them out and she heard him tasting her.

"Are you ready?" he whispered.

"Yes," she moaned. "Please Eric, please!"

She shuffled her knees apart an inch further, and then she felt him press against her, gasping at the first touch.

His cock was hard, and hot, nestling between the muscle of her tight ring like molten rock. He moved slowly and slightly at first, every single sensation causing her to mutter some utterance of pleasure, urging, and affirmation.

"Yes, yes!"

A thousand tiny confirmations of her own pleasure trickled from her mouth as he inched inside of her. Gasping as she felt her body opening up around his rigid length, the tight muscles of her ass relaxed as his lubricant-covered shaft glided inside of her with ease.

Eric tried to remain deathly mute. For him the sound of her body opening around him, and the sound of her pleasured moans were the most erotic things he'd ever heard. His shaft was halfway inside of her now, sliding in slowly, harder than iron steel.

She felt his fingers twinge around the curves of her hip, and cried as he pulled her back onto his cock.

"Oh baby, fucckk!" Her words were long and protracted, broken apart with shuddering gasps of her own hot breath. A smile was permanently plastered across her face. His fingers gripped tightly and he finished pulling inside of her. She felt his wide base bottom out against her flesh and her eyes flushed with black.

"You're so tight," he whispered from behind her.

"You're so big," she whispered back.

He drew his hips back, and then he pushed them forward, penetrating her properly for the first time. Claire's eyes screwed shut and her mouth opened, but no sound came. His fingers steeled against her waist and he started sliding back and forth, moving in and out of her with a steady rhythm now.

Her mouth rounded into the shape of a large O as he fucked her ass from behind. She heard the air being forced from his nose, relishing every squeeze from his thick finger tips.

"Do you have any idea..." he said as his thrusts became faster and more forceful, "how...fucking...beautiful...you are?"

With each word he dug inside of her deep and long, slipping back out quickly to do it all over again. Claire shuffled her knees apart once more, bringing a hand between her legs, pushing a finger between her folds, massaging her clit as he fucked her ass.

"Oh baby, oh fuck!"

Stars formed in her vision as she worked herself to a climax. The speed between them had picked up considerably now, and he was gliding in and out of her with ease, practically ramming his body against hers.

The corded muscles of his thighs slapped against her soft flesh, the thick base of his throbbing and veined cock tapped against her ass. His palms either gripped her tight, or smoothed circles on her ass, spanking her every now and then between thrusts.

Claire pushed her tits against the bed, finding pleasure at the friction from the covers. She pushed her ass up, opened her legs, and moved her hips back when he moved forward. She wanted it harder, deeper, faster—and he gave it.

She pushed her fingers inside of herself as his rhythm crested, his body slamming against her with quick and sharp thrusts.

"Oh baby!" she gasped. Her words were hardly words now, just breath trying to form the shape of vague sounds. With each thrust of his hips he caused a trickle of worship to escape from her lips.

"I'm coming," he whispered between hot breaths. "I'm coming, I'm coming."

"Yes," Claire begged, "Yes, yes!"

Her own orgasm came too, and she held her palm against her cunt, her clit throbbing as her pleasure exploded across her body. She felt his fingers squeeze into the fleshy curves of her hips and he yanked her back, pulling her all the way onto his length, burying his cock inside of her as deep as he could.

Her eyes bulged as she felt him erupt deep inside of her ass, his cock firing dozens of thick ropes up and into her cavity.

"Yes!" she cried. "Yes, yes, yes!"

She pushed herself back, urging for him to be deeper, urging for him to already fill the space that was completely full. He squeezed hard, more ropes of molten love squeezing from his head and coating her pink walls, until he had filled her almost completely.

The world melted away for Claire, and there was no other sensation than the feeling of him inside of her, filling her space completely. He stayed inside of her until he was completely done, and only then did he break away, falling into a heap on the bed beside her.

They lay in the dark together for the longest time, staring up at the ceiling, chests heaving as they regained their composure, sweat pouring from their bodies. Claire lay on her back looking up into the darkness, her forearm crossed over her head. The fingertips of his right hand were on top of her left thigh, just over her hips.

She closed her eyes and breathed deep, conscious of his warmth still inside of her. It felt good, it felt natural for it to be there. After a few minutes of silent appreciation, she turned her weight onto the side so she was facing him, moving one of her legs over his body so she was half-straddling him.

They kissed, a slow and lingering kiss, their lips parted, making the only noise in the room apart from their breathing.

"So," Eric said calmly. "What did you think?"

She smiled to herself, blinking slowly, looking down at the man with great appreciation.

"I liked it," she said, half giggling to herself. "*A lot.*"

"I'm glad," Eric said, brushing a hand through her hair. "Your body received me very well. I'm surprised at how fast you relaxed."

She drew her fingers down his chest, tracing the contours of his muscles with her hands.

"You've been teasing me for so long. Can you blame me?"

"I suppose not." Eric laughed.

"We need to do that again," Claire said. "Like, *a lot.* You probably need time to recover first though, right?"

Eric raised one eyebrow slowly.

"Will I really?"

Before Claire could realize what had happened, she was on her back with her legs in the air and Eric was kneeling over her, his hands on the back of her thighs.

She looked down and saw his hand around the meat of his cock. He was pressing his erection down, nestling the head in the muscles of her ring again.

"Eric, fuck!" She let out a sharp gasp as he penetrated her again, sliding his length inside of her slowly.

"One thing you'll come to learn about vampires, my darling." He pushed forward, filling her completely. "We've got great stamina."

CHAPTER EIGHT

Eric

THE FOUR VAMPIRES SAT TOGETHER AS THEY took council around the table. The stone room was dark, save for the dim light of the fire at the far end. On the table there were four glasses, three of which were empty. One still contained its blood.

Eric was dressed in his usual attire, black jeans and a black sweater. His father wore black trousers and a gray dress shirt, with the collar unbuttoned and the sleeves rolled up his scarred forearms. Sitting across from them were Will and Eli York. The brothers both wore old-fashioned suits. William's suit was a dark olive green, and Eli's was a midnight blue. Both brothers wore white shirts. Neither wore ties.

"Eric, Atticus. It's good to see you both. It's been a long time."

"Long enough to bury any misdoings your family have done in the past I hope?" Atticus stared into the dull emerald eyes of Will York, the older of the two brothers.

"Vampires are vampires," Will said coolly. "Unpredictable, irrational, passionate creatures. We make no apology for the treachery of our generations past. It's no secret the York family name was sullied by our fathers and their brothers. Rest assured, gentlemen, the apple falls far from the tree."

Eric shifted in his seat uncomfortably, holding the gaze of the two brothers with ease. "And if we were to take a bite of that apple, I should not be surprised to see that it's poisoned."

The brothers met Eric's cold remark with obliged silence. Atticus let out a sharp laugh, slapping his palm against the dark wood of the table between them.

"You'll have to forgive my son. He has a keen memory and a strong moral compass."

"I'm not a traitor, that's all you need to know," Eric spat, clarifying the matter for the York brothers.

"As neither are we," Eli, the younger of the two said. Although technically cousins by blood, Will and Eli York were known to all in the vampire world as brothers. Their fathers, Tyson and Nathaniel York, were infamous traitors, and their dark legacy loomed over the brothers like a shadow.

The treachery had never crossed the Belmont family directly, but it had affected some of their closest allies. Above all else, honor and trust were the two most important aspects to Eric. He knew little of the York brothers, but his perspective of them was tainted by their family's legacy. Until recently, the York family had been open enemies of the Belmont clan.

"We will do whatever it takes to prove we are not our fathers," Will clarified earnestly.

"You run to us with your tails between your legs," Eric said. "The White Order is smoking you from the hovel you call a home. You have no choice but to come to us."

"Exactly," Eli said. "And that is why we come to you in humility. We will do whatever it takes to get your help, and we will be in your debt. We are not humble creatures, Eric Belmont. It pains us to come to you on our knees like this. We hope to find a middle ground. If we do not work together, the White Order will be the end of us all."

The four vampires sat in silence for a moment, regarding the unfortunate truth of Eli's words. The visiting brothers were mirror images of each other: muted green eyes, with short ashen hair that curled slightly toward the ends. Their faces were broad and short, strong and handsome in a way that was distinctly different to the Belmont men.

Whereas Eric's complexion was pale white, Eli and William were more a pale gold. The brothers had full lips, which were starkly white in contrast to their faintly olive skin. Their cheekbones sat high on their face, and their emerald eyes sparkled beneath heavy lids that were full of ash-colored eyelashes. Will was the taller of the two, and his face was a little longer. Both brothers were clean-shaven, and their hair was short and neat. At a glance Will looked to be the brains, and the square-jawed Eli looked to be the brawn. Eric knew that both brothers were equally cunning, and he was unwilling to trust either. A long pink scar ran the length of Will's face.

"Well if that ain't the unfortunate truth," Atticus replied sadly. "The Order's strength has somehow grown considerably over the years. If we don't work to fight back against them, they will be the death of us."

Eric nodded, agreeing reluctantly with Eli's words. He cleared his throat and turned his eyes to the girl in the corner.

She stood silent with an arm folded over herself. Her eyes were large and dark. Her face was youthful, and timid. Her nose was small and in the cold it looked like a pink button. Her hair was jet black against her milk-white skin, falling in a long braid down the side of her body, which was frail and nimble. She wore a maid's uniform of some sort, a dark blue skirt accompanied by a white blouse. Her eyes were trained firmly on the floor. She reminded Eric of a scared field mouse.

"Who is she?" he said, motioning at the girl with his head. Eli and Will both looked back at the girl, then at each other, then back at Eric and Atticus. Eli's lips pulled tight across his mouth, his fists rolling slightly on the tabletop.

"Jessica," Will explained, looking at his brother from the corner of his eye. "She's is Eli's blood servant."

"Blood servant?" Eric laughed, looking at his father in bemusement. The York family had a reliance for blood, just as the Belmont family did, but their method of taking it was different. The York family had lived for generations with a family of humans, who were kept as blood slaves to York vampires. On the eve of their eighteenth birthday, the humans were given the choice of freedom or the choice to be turned.

"Why on earth would you bring a blood servant on a diplomatic mission?"

Eric raised an eyebrow, trying to figure it out. The behavior was highly unorthodox. Eric looked at Eli, who sat like a silent figure of torment. He could sense there was something going on there, but couldn't figure out what it was. Eli went to open his mouth but Will spoke for him once more.

"We realize it's unusual. But Eli's health has been strained as of late, and he needs access to blood at all times."

"We have blood here, you know," Atticus said. "State-of-the-art cooling system."

Atticus and Eric looked at the full glass of blood sitting in front of Eli.

"We realize that," Will continued. "But Eli only drinks from Jessica. We know it's unusual, but that's just how it is in our family."

Atticus and Eric both looked at the girl and Eli. They shared a passing glance of confusion before pressing on. Eric felt Jessica's gaze linger on him for the slightest moment, but didn't move his eyes to look at her again.

"Very well," Eric said. "So tell us what you want of the Belmont family. "What is it you need from us? And what will you give us in return?"

*

"This one is called the bird window," Sophia explained as they perched on the rounded sill of the large open window. "Because you can see most of the castle from its vantage."

Claire placed a hand on the cool stone ridge of the sill and gazed in awe upon the labyrinth of dark spires before her.

"It's so beautiful," she said. "I knew it was big, but I had no idea the castle was this big."

"It surprises me every day," Sophia admitted, turning from the window and carrying on down the passage. Claire walked after her, admiring the castle as they continued their tour.

"I've lived here all my life, but I still find parts of the castle every year that I've never been to before. We're in the Hollow now, it's neither old or new, quite in between."

The dark wooden floor creaked beneath their feet as they walked. Sophia led them down a set of giant stairs. Looking down, Claire could see they led into a large and open hall. "And this is the main entrance hall."

Claire's mouth gaped as they turned down flights until the wide and expansive stone floor of the entrance hall finally met their feet. Everywhere she looked there was beauty and art. Grand tapestries, giant portraits of Belmont family members gone past. The room was wide, tall, and open. A thousand candles filled the walls on each side, illuminating the peculiar darkness of the castle with a pleasant glow.

"It's one of the many entrances of course," Sophia explained. She brushed a hand through her dark black hair, and Claire smiled, thinking how much Sophia reminded her of a child. At the opposite end of the hall near the large wooden doors that almost ran the height of the room, there was a group of people. Sophia stopped dead in her tracks.

"Is everything all right?" Claire said, looking sideways at her tour guide.

"Yes... it's fine. I shouldn't have brought you down here. I forgot they were leaving today." Sophia's eyes remained fixed on the group just up ahead. Claire looked over too and saw the group were now looking back at them. By the door up ahead there were about half a dozen figures dressed in long black coats. Around them there was a vast collection of luggage and items. The group stared silently in the direction of Sophia and

Claire. Their backs were hunched, their faces gaunt and unpleasantly pale.

"One of the vampires that tried to attack you and Eric the other day was an elder for the Nash clan. Ever since Father learned of the attack, he has extinguished their family from our lineage."

There was that word again. Claire had heard Eric use the same word this morning when they'd parted ways.

"You've no need to fear walking these halls again," Eric had explained. *"Any traitors have been extinguished, and any others thinking of trying their luck have been given the message. It's safe."*

She had somehow found comfort in his words, and upon learning that Sophia wanted to give her a tour of the castle, she'd jumped at the chance. Eric was off on business with his father for part of the day, and she had nothing else to do, save fantasizing what she'd do with him when he got back.

"Yes," Sophia said. "Extinguished. It's a word my father doesn't use lightly, and I've certainly never heard him use it before."

"But what does it mean?" Claire asked. "Killed?"

Sophia looked at Claire and gave a brief yet frightened laugh. "Worse. There were two vampire families that tried to attack you yesterday. Rasputin Nash and a golem slave working for the Templemont clan. After learning of the attack, my father gave their families two options. Leave or be extinguished."

"Okay..."

"Extinguished means that every blood descendant of your line will be killed. The Nash family were smart enough to leave. The Templemonts said no."

"But what happened to them?"

Sophia looked at Claire but didn't speak. Her eyes seemed to say everything. Claire's eyes bulged in realization. The man she had met yesterday had been so mild-mannered and inviting.

"But Atticus..." Claire stammered.

"Seems so laid-back? Yes. That's where a lot of people underestimate his power. There's a reason the Nash family are leaving without a fight. We have to go this way. I guess I'll have to show you. Come on. Trust me. It'll be all right."

Sophia swallowed at something in her throat and marched across the hall. Claire followed quickly after her, her body feeling a little tense in anxiety. As they approached the group, the half-dozen or so members turned their eyes down to the floor and became deathly quiet.

They stepped aside to let Sophia and Claire pass, their eyes all the while fixed to the floor. Sophia led Claire through a smaller door that was etched into the giant hinged doors hanging above them. Once outside they both took a deep breath, the cool night air brushing over their faces.

Claire spoke first, her words leaping from her mouth with relief. "Holy hell, Sophia. That felt a little tense. What the heck was that?"

"Banished. All of them. They have been told under strict instruction to leave the Castle Belmont at once and never return. Father's words would have been sure to mention not to look at or talk to you. They're simply waiting here for a carriage to take them away. That's the last time you'll ever see them. Father clearly wants you to be safe here."

"Me? But why?"

"They threatened your life. You're a breeder. It's too rare a thing to throw away in some stupid power grab. Plus, besides that, you're one of us now."

"I'm one of *you?*"

Sophia giggled as she led Claire down a flight of stone steps that were cut into a dense garden of trees and flowers. "Well, yeah. You're part of the family, aren't you? I know Eric hasn't turned you or married you yet or anything but..."

Sophia trailed off, shrugging the rest of the sentiment away with her shoulders. Claire followed quickly behind her, her chest fluttering with the thought of everything Sophia had just promised. They walked through the gardens that surrounded the castle grounds, trailing along the delicately sculpted fauna, following a gray slate path down the side of the hill, Sophia narrating their tour all the while.

Claire was in love with the castle and its surrounding grounds, but her mind was preoccupied with thoughts of Eric, and whether or not she really was one of them now.

They followed the gray path around to the south side of the castle. The north and west sides were bordered with mountains; the east side was bordered with the deep ravine, under which the great black river ran. While the south side had more mountains, there was more distance between them and the castle, and there was a small space of flat land between the two.

"This is the main courtyard." She stopped and pointed back in the direction of the castle. "There's the old store elevator on this side that takes you back up as far as the twelfth floor. You have to use the stairs or walk across if want to get to any of the floors above that."

"I don't understand any of the floors in this place."

"You can be forgiven for being confused. I can appreciate it's probably confusing for a newcomer. All you have to remember is that the castle is old, and as the generations have gone by, new parts have been built on top of it...or even under it. Which isn't helpful."

They walked down a set of stone steps, past a water fountain, and down onto a track that hugged the cliff wall at the edge of the castle.

"That's not exactly helpful! I'm on the ninth floor with Eric, but I went down nine flights and somehow ended up on the twelfth floor?"

Sophia nodded. "The part of the castle that you and Eric are in is one of the older ones. A few hundred years after it was built our ancestors built another twelve floors underneath and connected the structures. So floor nine in Eric's part of the castle is more like floor twenty-one." She stopped at seeing the confused look on Claire's face. "There's not going to be a quiz on any of this! Don't worry!"

They both burst into laughter. "I'm glad," Claire said. "Where are you taking me now anyway?"

She looked up at the steep rock face on either side of her.

"This is the little secret that's hidden underneath the Castle Belmont."

The track ended at a small wooden door which had a solitary silver ring upon it. Sophia pulled out a key and opened the door. Inside she pushed a button on the wall and a second later a line of torches illuminated all around them, revealing a large underground cavern, filled with smoking pools of water.

"I'm sure Eric has told you that we don't fare too well with technology." Sophia ushered Claire in and closed the door behind them. "We tried to get a heated pool installed once but it kept breaking. A few years ago we were doing some excavations and we found this place almost by accident."

They walked to the edge of the water and Sophia knelt. "Put your hand in."

Claire did and was delighted to find the water was the perfect temperature for bathing. "My goodness! It's so warm! It's perfect!"

"Right?!" Sophia stood up smiling. "We got Ira to install some torches down here and we've been using it as a bathing spot ever since."

"But...I thought vampires couldn't feel heat?" Claire said, turning her thumb in her fingers. Sophia laughed once more.

"We can't really. We can feel a slight amount, but it still makes all the difference. I don't know what it is, but there's something about these waters. They have a way of making you feel good as new. What do you say? Feel like a splash?"

"Oh, I haven't got a bathing suit with me," Claire said.

"So?" Sophia stripped off in front of Claire as if it were nothing and a moment later she had jumped into the bubbling water. Claire looked around the cavern, incredulous.

"But what if people come?! What if people see me naked?"

"It's just skin, Claire." Sophia shrugged. "Besides, I'm the only one who ever comes down here anyway. Barely anyone else has a key."

Claire nodded. "Well, you make a compelling point. And that water does look great."

Claire stripped, folded her things and placed them in a neat pile on the floor, next to Sophia's crumbled pile of clothes. She lowered herself gingerly into the water, sighing with great relief as she felt every ounce of stress melt away instantly.

"So." Sophia stared at Claire with a huge smile plastered on her face. "Tell me what life was like before you came to the castle."

*

"It's simply ridiculous!" Eric stood from the table and walked across the room, resisting the temptation to stake the two idiots that had been beset before him. "You're asking too much, too soon. If you'd known things were this bad, you should have come and asked for help sooner, or you should have left your home altogether."

"It's not that simple, Eric," Will said defiantly. "We can't just leave Blackstone. It's our home. There are five generations of York vampires living there."

"How did the White Order come to gain such a strong foothold in your part of the country?" Atticus asked. "There were a few breakaway factions here, but we took care of them with little effort."

"They're not like other factions that we have encountered," Eli said. "Vampires have dealt with hunting societies like the White Order since the dawn of time. Those fools aren't content to rest until every last one of us is dead and buried in the ground."

"We're all familiar with the White Order and their motives," Eric said. "What my father asked still stands. Why are they troubling you so? Is your family really so weak that you can't handle a troupe of renegade vampire hunters?"

Will York stood from the table, clenching his fists. Eric was pushing him, and he could tell that he was on the last string of his patience. Will took a deep breath. He knew that if he snapped, he would lose all chance of gaining help from the Belmont clan.

"It's not that we are weak," Will explained. "But they are absurdly strong."

"They're only human," Atticus said. "Surely your physical strength outpaces them tenfold?"

"You'd think so," Eli interjected. "But it's not the case. There's something different about them. We think they have a witch, and we think they are working with a local shifter troupe as well."

Both Eric and Atticus felt ice pass over their bodies at the mention of shifters.

"Shifters? Werewolves?"

Will and Eli nodded solemnly.

"Can you prove this?"

The brothers thought for a second. Eli spoke first. "There is no—"

"We have proof," Will said. Eli shot a furtive glance at his brother as if to silence him.

"We do not," Eli hissed at Will.

"If you want our help," Eric said, "you will show us the proof. We will not rise to assist you with the White Order alone. But if you are fighting shifter kin, I feel compelled to step forward and help."

Atticus nodded, mirroring his son's sentiment. "Our families may have had difficulties in the past, but we are united in one thing. Our hatred for the shifter kin."

Eric brought a thumb and finger to the bridge of his nose at the very thought of the wretched kin. He had never understood the disparaged relationship shared by their kind. All he knew was that shifter kin were dangerous, and the two kinds were destined to hate each other for all time.

Eli took a deep breath before turning back to his blood servant in the corner. "Jessica, darling, come here."

Darling? Eric held Eli's words in his ear in bemused regard. There was definitely some kind of affectionate relationship going on between this vampire and his blood servant, which was unheard of to Eric.

The young girl nervously stepped forward from out of the shadows.

"Tell them what happened at the ridge that night."

All eyes in the room shifted to the face of Jessica. Fear flashed through the young girl's face seemingly at the memory. Eli brushed a hand down her arm in reassurance. "It's okay. You're not there now, you're here with me. You're safe. I need you to tell Eric and Atticus what happened that night."

Jessica stared at Eli for a long moment, and Eric could sense a deep warmth flaring in the space between their eyes.

However unconventional their relationship might be, it was clear to Eric that the young girl meant a lot to Eli, and him to her in turn.

She pulled her eyes from her master and her gaze fell squarely on Eric.

"I had finished working in Blackstone for the day. I was on my way back from the letting parlor to the servant chambers. It's connected usually, but there was a storm last winter, and part of the house became damaged. It's nothing really, but it means we servants had to take a short detour outside to get back to our quarters. I was on my own. It was night. The moon was out. That was when I saw him up on the hill. He was a man—and then he wasn't. Then he attacked me. I nearly died. I would have, were it not for Eli..."

She broke off from the story, her words and the angst-ridden expression on her face tale enough that the wasn't lying. The girl's whole body trembled in remembrance of the ordeal. A solitary track of tears rolled down her face and Eli grabbed her, pulling her into his grasp.

"It's all right, Jessica. It's okay. You're safe, I'm here...I'm here."

Eli cooed the girl gently back to normalcy. Eric and Atticus stood on the edges of their feet, staring at each other, unsure.

"I don't doubt what happened, Eli. But we need evidence of this, you understand. We can't just go off the words of a blood servant."

The brothers looked at each other as if they were lost for words.

"We can't prove any more than this, old man," Will said with disappointment hinged on his voice. "This is all we have."

"Actually," Jessica's voice broke the silence this time, causing everyone to stare at her. "It isn't."

The young servant pulled herself free from the reassuring grasp of her master.

"Jessica, no!" Eli reached after the girl, but she pushed his hand away.

"It's all right, Eli. I'm not scared anymore."

Without saying another word, the servant girl turned from the group and pulled her shirt up, over the tops of her narrow shoulder blades. She slipped her arms from the sleeves, and unfastened the clasp to her bra, holding it firmly against the front of her body.

Drawn down the length of her back were four deep scars, white lines broken across the pink expanse of her otherwise flawless flesh. The paw of the offending beast must have easily been four times the size of a normal wolf. The cuts raked from the top of the spine all the way to the bottom, veering off to the left just at the end.

"That's the mark of a shifter all right," Atticus nodded. "I've seen enough in my time to know what those bastards can do." Atticus turned to Eric. "What do you reckon?"

"I've only been in battle with them up close once, but it certainly looks real to me."

Jessica redressed quietly, while the vampires held each other in silent regard. Will was the first to speak, finally breaking the silence.

"So," he said. "Can we count on your help then?"

Eric and Atticus shared a glance with each other. Even though Eric knew the choice was ultimately up to his father, power would be succeeding to him soon, and his father wanted Eric to start taking lead on things. He saw the look in his father's eye, nodded, and faced the brothers once more.

"We'll help," he said finally. "But I have things that I have to attend to here first. I'll need a week or two, and then I'll come. And I'll bring help."

"No Wraith. That bastard is more crazy than help," Will said.

"Trust me," Atticus interjected. "I know shifters and I know Wraith. You want all the crazy you can get."

The meeting broke finally, and the York clan were back on the road again within an hour of leaving the table with Atticus and Eric.

"It's serious business you're getting into," Atticus said to his son. "You understand any vampire that goes on this expedition may die."

"I do," Eric said flatly. "But what I said stands. Will and Eli may be scared of the White Order first, but I know the real truth. Men are men. I will deal with them as they come. The real threat is that of the shifter kin. The Yorks are only a few hundred miles from us. If we start allowing shifter kin to run around unchecked..." A shiver passed over him.

"It won't be long before they start cropping up here."

"Exactly," Eric said.

After reviewing the meeting briefly with his father, Eric was away again, returning once more back into the castle to find Sophia and Claire. They had arranged that morning to meet at

Sophia's room on the fifth floor at the end of the night, but once Eric got there he found they were nowhere to be seen.

There was no fear in his stomach this time, for he knew that Sophia would keep Claire in good company, but she was often late—and he always came to expect delays whenever Sophia was involved. As they weren't coming to him, he would try and seek them out, but finding a solitary inhabitant of the castle was a task easier said than done. He decided to go and pay Ira a visit first at the blood banks. After he'd quenched his thirst, he'd find Claire, and pick up right where they left off.

Thoughts of his curvy mate had stalked through Eric's mind all night, and had been at the forefront of his thoughts, right up until the troubling meeting he'd had with the York brothers. Despite the serious nature of the conversation, Claire had stepped back into his mind's eye as soon as the meeting was done. Even as he sat in Ira's waiting room for blood, she danced in his imagination, wearing little else but scant lingerie, tempting and teasing every fiber of his being. He sat in the room, far removed from its walls, floating a thousand miles away with thoughts of Claire, and thoughts of what he'd do with her once he had her alone again that night.

"I said hi, Eric!"

A blow sunk into his arm and Eric shook his head, pulling himself from his daydream and back into the waiting room. He was disappointed to see a blonde and scantily clad female vampire stood in front of him.

"Oh, hey Lana," Eric said flatly.

"Oh come on, Mr. Belmont!" Lana threw herself down beside Eric and batted her long black lashes. "You can do better than that. There was a time when you were running after me along with all the other boys in the castle."

"Actually, there wasn't—you're getting me mixed up with Wraith." Eric picked a magazine up off the side and thumbed through it to try and show Lana that he wasn't interested in talking. The gesture seemed to madden the blonde. Eric had grown up with Lana and he knew the tyrant well. She was the eldest daughter and heir to the Cavotti vampire line, and she had spent the last several decades vying for Eric's attention.

"Whatever." Lana threw a hand through her blonde hair and placed a hand on Eric's shoulder. "What have you been up to these days? I feel like I haven't seen you in forever. It is true that you're going around telling everyone you've got some dumb human girl as a mate? Such a dumb rumor. We should go out hunting sometime. Veronica and I found this great little town just an hour south of here..."

"I'm not interested." Eric stood up, throwing the magazine down onto the table. He needed blood, but he knew he couldn't sit here and listen to the vapid blonde rattle on any longer. Eric was about to duck behind the counter to see exactly what the hell was taking Ira so long when he remembered he'd had three days' of personal supply brought up to the chiller in his bedroom on the ninth floor.

"I'm such an idiot," he said to himself quietly. He turned around to leave and saw Lana staring at him expectantly. There were half a dozen other vampires in the waiting room, all of whom had their eyes glue to Lana. The other vampires in Castle Belmont might have fallen for Lana's good looks, but Eric couldn't care less. As far as he was concerned she was the devil in a blonde wig. Lana did things that made Wraith look like a puppy.

"What do you want?!" Eric hissed.

"I said do you want to go hunting this weekend? Veronica and I have found a great spot."

"No." Eric shook his head. "The rumors you heard are true. I've got a mate, and she's human."

Eric pushed past Lana, his shoulder turning her body as he went. Lana scoffed at his rejection and swathed her hair once more.

"Ugh. Human mate!? Gross! There's no way she looks anything like me!"

Eric stopped and turned, his eyes firing daggers at the leggy blonde. Lana saw blood in his eyes and her smile dropped immediately.

"You're right," he said. "She looks nothing like you."

Lana looked shocked for a moment, then she smiled and her eyebrows danced, as if she were flattered.

"She's beautiful. And you're ugly. Ugly as you are on the inside. She's nothing like you and she never will be, and that's why I love her."

The words stunned Lana into silence, along with the rest of the room. Eric's admission even stunned himself for half a second. He glowered at Lana, whose mouth was stammering in effort to say something in return. It was to Eric's satisfaction that the mouthy blonde had nothing to say for what must have been the first time ever.

He turned on his heels and thundered out of the room without another word.

*

As Claire retold her life before Castle Belmont, Sophia sat in the water quietly, listening intently to her words. Claire skirted around some details, giving Sophia the basics of who she was and what her life was before she came here. As always, her thoughts of her previous life were vague. She was already looking ahead to her future with an eagerness, putting as much distance between her past and present as possible.

"It's beautiful down here," Claire said, trying to shift the focus of conversation away from her. "I almost feel like I'm in some luxury hotel."

"We did think about getting a steam room and a sauna fitted," Sophia joked. "But even Atticus drew the line at that one. Looks like we've still got plenty of time until we're due back to see Eric. I could show you the blood bank, but something tells me you wouldn't be so interested in seeing that."

"Blood bank?" Claire swallowed.

"It's not nearly as tragic as it sounds. Both Eric and myself are something of an anomaly here at Castle Belmont. Most other vampires tend to hunt their food. We lost the taste for such activities a long time ago."

"But how does it work? Do you need blood to live?"

"Unfortunately. We have tried to go without it, tried to reduce our intake—but it's no good. The side-effects are too numerous. Headaches, nausea, trembling."

"Sounds similar to the symptoms of people who go through addiction withdrawal."

"So I've been told." Sophia's eyes flitted down to the ground and her smile faltered. She paused for a moment before looking back at Claire. "You never mentioned your family."

"Huh?"

"When you were talking about your life just now. You never mentioned your family once. You mentioned you were a nurse, you mentioned you lived alone and that you wanted children— but you didn't mention anything about family."

Claire stared down into the water, studying the reflection of the torches as they danced on the rippling black canvas. "I was always something of a black sheep. An outcast. I was always an outsider to them for some reason."

Sophia sat in expectant silence, daring Claire to go on.

"I don't know why," she said. "But my parents always loved my sister so much more than me. And I know I wasn't imagining it. She was their obvious favorite. I love my sister Lisa, and I think she loves me to an extent, but I always felt like I was on the outside looking in."

"I'm sorry," Sophia said. A smile came over her face. "Maybe you were just waiting to find your real family?"

Claire smiled at her words and she felt a warmth spread inside her at that thought. She thought that maybe her place really was here with Eric at Castle Belmont. "Maybe." She smiled and looked across the cavern.

"What about you, Sophia? You certainly seem to have an eclectic family. Do you like it here at the castle? How long have you been here?"

"Our family first settled in this castle in the seventeenth century, but we tend to move around quite a bit. I was actually born in Florence, and we spent much of my childhood traveling around Europe. When I reached adulthood Father said it was time for him to return back to Castle Belmont. He said the rest of us were free to move about as we wished, but we must return to the castle once a year to stay within the family favor, and we have to carry out our duty when it is required of us."

"Duty?"

"It can mean many different things." Sophia rolled her eyes and waved a hand. "For the most part it's not something that comes up that often."

"So there's Eric, Wraith, and you?"

"And Veronica," Sophia reminded her. "My oldest sister. You'll meet her at some point. She's... not like me, but she's no Wraith either. It's been a while since we've all lived together in one place. I think now that Father is getting older, it is important for us to be here, as the reins transfer over to Eric."

"And what about *your* love life, Sophia?" Claire smiled. "Is there anyone special out there for you? Or someone in the castle perhaps?"

Melancholy seemed to wash across Sophia's face and her smile disappeared quickly. "There was maybe, once. I'm not so sure anymore."

Claire sensed that the topic was sensitive for Sophia and she decided to move on from it. "Well, if Veronica is anything like you I'm sure she's a treasure. You're certainly the nicest vampire I've met so far."

Sophia smiled, some of the happiness returning to her face. "Veronica is okay. She can be a bit of a nightmare sometimes. Of all my brothers and sisters Eric is my favorite. Wraith is... well. Wraith is Wraith."

"Was he always like this?" Claire asked, thinking back to the brief but horrific entanglement she'd had with the man.

"Who, Wraith? Oh heavens no." Sophia sat up straight, puzzlement upon her face. "Didn't...didn't Eric tell you what happened to him?"

"No? Whatever do you mean?"

Sophia looked around the cavern as if to check no one was listening in on their conversation. She leaned in as if to whisper a deadly secret to Claire when an alarm sprang from over Claire's shoulder.

"Christ!" They both jumped at the noise. Claire turned around and grabbed her phone from her pile of clothes, silencing the alarm. Claire looked down at the time on her phone, seeing that they were late for their meeting with Eric.

"That was the alarm for meeting Eric back at your room. It was supposed to go off a half hour ago. We're late!" Claire hurriedly climbed from out of the pool, Sophia following quickly behind.

"Oh crap." Sophia ran to the wall and grabbed two towels for them both to dry off. "I must have messed it up with undead mumbo jumbo. I'm sorry!"

"It's all right. Thanks." Claire grabbed a towel from Sophia and they both dried themselves down, hurriedly changing back into their clothes.

"Come on then. Let's hurry back to my room. Hopefully Eric is still waiting for us there. I don't like to keep my brother waiting. He's patient but I don't want to keep him from you. He gets a temper when he's kept from his Claire..."

Claire laughed to herself as Sophia locked the door to the caverns behind them. She felt a strange sense of pride whenever she heard people talking about how protective Eric was over her.

They walked back up through the gardens of the castle, into the main walls through one of the many side entrances.

"I must say I'm looking forward to having a little niece or nephew."

Claire heard Sophia's words, and for the first time the idea struck her that if all things went to plan, she would be pregnant with Eric's child at some point in the coming weeks. She had been so preoccupied with exploring his body, and letting him explore hers, that she'd completely forgotten about the end goal of their coming together. Eric had abducted her in the first place for the suitability of her womb.

"I don't understand any of this... 'breeder' stuff," Claire said as they walked through the castle back to Sophia's room. "How does Eric know that I'm a breeder? When will we be able to..." She trailed off at the end of the sentence, unwilling to question Eric's own sister on the nature of their sex life.

"You'll know soon," Sophia said, half-blushing in realization at the delicacy of the topic. "As for knowing if you're a breeder or not, it's pretty obvious to vampires of the opposite sex if a human is a breeder or not. Our senses are much higher than that of humans, and apparently breeders are absolutely enticing to vampires."

"Well, that would explain why he can never keep his hands off me," Claire joked. Then her face flushed with mortification as she realized what she had said to Eric's sister. "Oh goodness, I'm so sorry!"

"It's all right!" Sophia giggled. "To be honest I have a morbid curiosity about it all. I don't really want to know what you guys have been up to while you've been here of course, but this is all as new to me as it is to you and Eric. The last time there was a breeder in the castle was when my mother was here, and that was over twenty years ago. We haven't seen one since."

"So you never knew her?" Claire asked. "She died before you were born?"

"Mother? Heavens no, I knew her for the better part of a century..."

Claire's eyes widened at Sophia's admission. "Of course." She shook her head. "I'm constantly forgetting age doesn't affect vampires the same way. I've been thinking of you as the same age as me."

Sophia smiled. "It's okay, I'll take it as a compliment. As for this breeder stuff, the one person you'll be best asking is Ira... and hey! Speak of the devil!"

As they rounded the top of a staircase Claire and Sophia were faced with the Victorian-clad doctor. Ira stood with a book to his eyes, studying the words intensely as he stood in the middle of the corridor.

"Ira, hey!" Sophia called out to the doctor and approached him eagerly. Claire followed closely behind.

"Huh? What?" Ira turned his head at the last moment in an almost languid shock. "Oh! Sophia! Claire!" The two vampires kissed air and Ira tucked the thick leather tome beneath his arm.

"What are you two lovely women up to tonight?"

"I was just giving Claire a tour of the grounds and the pools," Sophia sang.

"Ah, most fascinating!" Ira beamed, rocking on his heels. "I trust Master Eric is treating you fair Claire? Is everything going all right with your consummation?"

Things were going *very* well. That was what Claire wanted to say. She'd had more orgasms in the last week then she'd had in her entire life. She stammered, stalling for her brain to conjure up a more diplomatic answer.

"Things are going great actually, thanks. Eric is a royal tease."

Ira beamed at her words, knowing full well what she meant. "Ah yes! Well, it's all part of the process you see. We need to make sure that you're ready for the best chance..." Ira trailed off at the end of his sentence, and his eyes rapidly flicked down over Claire's body. Claire barely noticed the gesture, but there was something about it that made her feel uneasy.

"In fact, Ira, there were a few things I've been meaning to ask you about the whole process—"

"Well my dear, there's a book in the library I can get you should you need instruction..."

"No," Claire laughed. "Not help with that. Just...how do I know when I'll be ready? Eric keeps saying I'll know when I'll know, but what does that mean?"

"Ah yes. Well... from reading the journals of Belladonna, I am familiar with the subject somewhat. She detailed her sessions in rather explicit detail, and even though her breeder was a *male*, I believe the sensations are the same for both parties regardless."

"So, is there anything I can expect? Some telltale sign to let me know when I'm ready?"

"There was one passage I remember in particular," Ira said, pushing his glasses up to the bridge of his nose. "Where the Lady Belladonna describes herself going into a heightened frenzy of passion. If I can recall verbatim she described it so:

'My libido has swelled to a great ocean of fire, which rages across my skin like lashes of flame. My whole body tingles with itching heat, and my mind craves nothing else other than to feel the flesh of my lover sheathed between the cup of my red flower. My eyes burn to see him, my mouth burns to kiss him, my hands burn to touch.'"

Ira coughed gently, indicating that he had finished his recollection.

"Well..." Claire felt her face blushing once more.

"Quite the vivid picture," Sophia said with one eyebrow raised.

"Quite! I can fetch the journal from the archives if you like?"

"No, it's all right," Claire smiled. "We best be going anyway, Ira. Eric is expecting us, but thank you for your words."

They said goodbye to the doctor and continued down the hall. As they walked Claire looked back and caught the doctor staring at her once more. A chill passed over her and she ran forward a few paces to catch up to Sophia.

They reached Sophia's room a few minutes later. Upon arriving there, there was no sign of Eric, so they decided to wait, assuming that he would be back there at some point. Sophia sat Claire at her dressing table, braiding her hair while she stood behind her. As she decorated Claire's hair in all manners of fancy, they made idle chitchat as they waited for Eric.

"The journal was funny, aye? Was it any use to you?"

Claire smiled at Sophia in the mirror.

"Perhaps. Her language was certainly... *descriptive,* that's for sure."

They laughed together, and fell into a peaceful silence, Claire almost feeling half-drowsy as Sophia's nimble fingers danced through her hair, twisting it into a thing of beauty.

"You're good at this."

"Decades of practice."

As Sophia worked her magic on Claire's hair, Claire stared into the mirror at the girl looking back at her, the girl who was so different from the one she had been just a week ago. She thought of the words in Belladonna's journal, the description of skin burning like fire as a sign of a breeder being ready. She brought her mind to the dull sensation of heat across her own body, the sensation she had first noticed when she had woken this morning. It was nothing like the description in the journal, but it was definitely something, and Claire knew that it meant the end of her release was near.

She closed her eyes and saw her lover standing before her. She removed his clothes and pushed him back onto black velvet, spreading her legs as she mounted him, pushing him inside of her, groaning as she felt him fill her completely.

The space between her legs tingled as she sat on the chair, unable to draw her thoughts to anything else. Prickles of heat flared across her skin as she thought of Eric, rising steadily with each moment. Her body was starting to burn for him, and soon, he would mount her, whether he thought she was ready or not.

CHAPTER NINE

Claire

"I trust Sophia hasn't only subjected you to mischief." Eric brushed a hand down Claire's arm and planted a neat kiss on her forehead as they were reunited. They had eventually reconvened outside Sophia's room, and after a brief chat with his sister, Eric thanked her for keeping Claire safe, and they left to return to his room.

"Quite the contrary," Claire said. "She gave me a tour of the castle, and we even bathed in the hot springs beneath the castle grounds."

Eric raised an eyebrow in surprise. "Fancy. I'm glad you had a good time."

"It was lovely, thank you. How was your business? I know you weren't looking forward to the meeting." Claire could sense that Eric had been reluctant about the family "business" that he'd been summoned to earlier that morning.

"It was hard work, but it's done now. Another family came to us asking for our assistance. I didn't want to help, but they presented some damning evidence. I'm afraid I have no choice. I will have to help them in a few weeks."

"Oh...okay." Claire's eyes dropped to the ground in sadness.

"I'm sorry," Eric said, sighing quietly to himself. "I promise it won't be for long, and we still have time with each other before then. I will make sure Sophia and Veronica keep you safe."

"But what about the castle, what about the other families, what about..."

"Wraith? He is to come with me. He has a... particular set of skills and they are needed for this task. As for the other families, you have my word that they won't bother you again."

They walked in silence for a few moments before Claire broached the subject that had been running through her mind since Sophia had brought it up.

"Sophia mentioned something to me earlier. About Wraith. She said that he hadn't always been this way."

Eric pulled Sophia close to him and immediately placed a finger over her lips.

"Quiet." He looked up and down the corridor. "I know I promised I would talk to you of such things, but now is not the time nor place. Come, we're only a few minutes from my room—we can discuss it there. I promise."

When they returned to Eric's room, he locked the door behind them and took a deep breath.

"Come, sit on the bed. I will explain everything."

Claire did as he asked, watching Eric as he paced back and forth. He brushed his hands through his hair as he walked, as if he were recounting the details of some important story. He looked tense, and agitated.

"We don't have to talk about it if you don't want to."

"No. We do. It's the Belmont family secret, and you're one of us now, so it's important that you know."

Eric crouched in front of Claire and took her hands in his own.

"You have to pledge to me that you won't share this information with anyone else, however. No one outside the family knows. Only Father, Veronica, Sophia, and I."

"I promise you Eric, I swear. What is it?"

"Wraith was normal once upon a time. For the first part of our life while we were growing up, we were inseparable. Back when I was young and wild, we loved to hunt together. I was probably the worst of the two. All was well with life. We had scraps as brothers do, but we were normal, we were happy. As happy as vampires can be anyway."

"So he was like you are now?"

"Kind of," Eric said, half turning away before looking back. "You have to understand that I wasn't always the person you see before you today. Not all vampires are like I am. Hunting brings something out in us. If you do it enough, that other side becomes your permanent face. We become cold, distant, cruel. My sister Veronica, she still has a shred of decency, but a few more decades and she will be wild with cruelty."

"Okay..."

"I made efforts to change myself. Sophia was born innocent, she was born pure. She never liked to hunt for game. So I changed for her. That creature you met the night I brought you here, that was a mere taste of my old self. You helped break it again, and bring me back to my improved self. Well, the old

Wraith was hardly a saint, but he was a damn sight better than he was now."

"What happened?"

"First of all, you have to understand that there is strange magic in this world. Vampires are but the tip of the iceberg. There are other creatures out there, for more mysterious than I. Wizards, witches, demons..."

"Demons?"

"Yes." Eric hung his head. "And is that very affliction that curses Wraith to this day."

"I don't understand."

"Our old home was in Europe, and we had many happy years there. My mother died under mysterious circumstances— circumstances that are still unclear to this day."

"I'm sorry."

"It's okay. It was a long time ago. After her death, a melancholy swept over our family, and a dark energy seemed to take over our house. It went like that for months, until weird things started happening."

"Weird things? Like what?"

"Strange creatures appeared, strange and dark creatures that were attracted to our melancholy. Demons, you see, they are like magnets. They are drawn to negative energy, and they set upon the house like a flock. It took us some time to realize what was happening, and when we did realize we decided to fight back. Small darkness attracts large darkness, and large darkness attracts death."

"And then what?"

"We fought back the only way we knew how—with our fists. A local clan of shifter folk had moved in." Eric paused at the confusion on Claire's face. "Werewolves for lack of a better word."

Claire nodded slowly.

"They're drawn to the energy just as the shadows are, and they had taken residence in our valley. Wraith and I set to work on cleaning the pack out. It was up on the mountain, on the very last night of our mission when it happened. We had found their main hiding spot and we were clearing them out. It was hard work but we succeeded, and I felt a shift in the energy immediately."

"You had won over the melancholy?"

"Almost, but mother nature doesn't like to go out with a whimper. She goes out with a bang. The heavens opened up and a storm the likes of which I've never seen came down upon the earth. Flashes filled the night air, as lightning struck down a hundred times a minute. Wraith and I were running back to the house for our lives. He was just ahead of me when I saw it happen. There was an almighty bang and the earth exploded underneath him. Next thing I knew, he was facedown on the grass, still as death.

"He was hit?"

Eric nodded. "I thought he had died instantly. I picked him up and carried him home and laid him on the table before Father. We were planning funeral arrangements when his eyes opened again."

"So he was all right?"

"Yes and no. He was alive, but he wasn't Wraith any longer. As it turns out, the storm wasn't a regular storm, it was a shadow storm, a rare paranormal phenomenon—the result of a dark portal opening in the skies above the earth. The flashes that filled the valley, they weren't forks of lightning. They were the paths of demons trying to get to earth."

Claire sat wordless, trying to understand the implications of Eric's story.

"But why did the portal open?"

"To this day we don't know," Eric sighed. "They are vary rare and extremely dangerous. It was probably brought about by the final surges of melancholy as we made an effort to fight back against it. We suspect it's somehow connected to whatever killed my mother in the first place."

Claire blinked, and Eric felt the need to go on.

"When Wraith was hit, his body was taken over by a demon. The morning after the storm, the melancholy had left our house, and Father decided we should move back to America. Wraith was never the same. Whatever dark entity had taken over his soul left him cruel, dark, and completely amoral. He's never been the same since. The demon lies dormant in him, but it taints his very soul. He is Shadow Cursed."

Silence beat between them, as Claire felt a strange sadness wash over her. The same creature that she had feared, hated, and felt repulsed by, was the same creature that she now felt sorry for.

"In a way it was almost like he sacrificed himself," Claire said. "To help defeat the dark energy that had taken over your family."

Eric nodded. "We have looked the world over for some sort of cure, but there is none. There are no others that know of the Belmont family secret, for it could be incredibly dangerous in the hands of others. If other vampires knew that Wraith was really possessed, they could try and harness his power, using the demon within him. No one else knows, not Ezra, not Ira. Only us. You have to keep this with yourself."

"I will." Claire gripped her lover's hand tightly. "I promise. Thank you for sharing it with me."

"You deserve to know," Eric said. "I should have told you sooner when you had your run-in with Wraith. There is a reason for his behavior. Maybe we should have killed him a long time ago, but I have never found the strength to do it."

"Why is this knowledge so dangerous?" Claire asked.

"To be Shadow Cursed... it is a powerful thing. Wraith's body harbors the raw energy of the demon inside of him. Demons aren't of this earth, and they can't live here long without a vessel in which they can hide. Normally it is humans that are Shadow Cursed. It would happen to sailors out at sea back in the past. The men would go wild with the power and kill everyone on board. Their own strength was amplified by the power of the demon inside of them."

"But a Shadow Cursed vampire..." Claire muttered, half speaking to herself.

"Exactly," Eric said. "The power of a vampire is already multitudes stronger than that of a man. I've seen rare glimpses of the demonic power that Wraith possesses. But when I see it... my God." Eric's eyes glazed over. "I've never seen power like it before. If Wraith knew what he was capable of, if he only knew the strength that lies inside of him..."

"You mean he doesn't know?!"

Eric shook his head. "At least... I don't think. We've only seen it once or twice, and when he comes back, he seems to have no memory. One thing is clear: one day the demon will wake up for good."

"And then what?" Claire said, almost hanging off the edge of her seat. "What will happen?"

"I don't know," Eric answered honestly. "But I don't want to be around to find out."

*

Claire and Eric quickly fell back into their old routine. Once they were reunited, they didn't part for several days. Day melded into night, and night faded into day, blurring together in an obscure stretch of time that seemed to ebb in both directions. They remained in Eric's room, with the blinds closed and the door bolted shut. The only disturbance came once in the morning and once at night, to deliver food for Claire and chilled vials of blood for Eric.

"I've missed you," Claire gasped as his warm and full lips traced down her neck and into the line of her cleavage. Eric growled back in response while biting her flesh softly.

"I can tell," he purred, squeezing her breast in his hand while he sucked at her nipples with his lips. Claire sank her fingers into the thick brown hair on his head, pulling him tight as his lips left sparks on her body. He rolled his hips against her as he said the taunting words, pressing the outline of his long cock against her warm and wet hollow.

They were naked minutes later, and he had carried her across to the bed. He laid her down gently at first, as if she were some delicate flower. He crawled onto the bed after her, he pulled and twisted her body around like a feral caveman, moving her into new positions as their bodies moved together in ever changing combinations. She loved it most when his hands would sink around her waist and pull her down the mattress to meet him, or when he'd place his palms on the insides of her thighs and push them apart with gentle force. Everything he did ignited fire inside her, making her body tingle with need for him.

She begged for him to take her fully, daily, yet he resisted. Claire often entertained the idea of throwing some sort of petulant fit, and thought about withholding sex from him altogether until he'd give her what she wanted, but she knew she wouldn't be able to follow such torture.

They did just about everything else however, and she grew to love the sensation of his cock pulsing in and out of her ass, almost longing after it with a fevered addiction. They fucked until they both reached aching climaxes, pulled away to rest and kiss each other tenderly, and then they'd come together again, fucking in a whole new position, finding parts of each other's body that were new and exciting.

She would straddle him, holding his thick shaft tight in her small hand as she sank down onto him, gasping as she felt the meat of his steel cleaving her tight hole in two. It gave her great pleasure in watching his face writhe and twist in ecstasy underneath her as she would roll her hips gently, sliding up and down his shaft until he could take no more.

It would be at that point that he'd fling his hands around her waist and take control of the pace, holding her still while his cock thundered in and out of her. Claire would place one hand against her breasts and the other against her pussy, rolling her head back as she squatted over him still, her body quaking in pleasure from orgasm after orgasm.

Then there were the times when he'd be on top, his large barbarian hands around her calves, pushing them back and holding them still while he thrust inside of her, long and slow. She would bite her lip, close her eyes, and roll them around her skull while his hands played with her clit. He would go slow, fast, gentle, hard—always changing and always keeping her guessing until another orgasm would surely come.

And of course, there was when he was behind her, either lying together on their sides, his hand smoothing over her bulbous hips while his cock slid into her gently, or on their knees, with her whole body lurching back at every thrust, aching for him to be as deep as possible.

There were all these positions and more, as they explored one another's bodies and brought them together in a multitude of positions. They found new ways to bring each other pleasure all the time, cresting together in a heaping pile of sweat and love until they could take it no more. Some hours he'd simply hold one hand flat against the flesh of her sex while his tongue worked miracles on her, flitting in small circles or long arching strokes, building up pressure inside of her until she'd come, screaming into the quiet of the night.

They bathed together, lathering every inch of each other's bodies completely, rinsing, drying each other off, then moving back to the bed and doing it all over again, until they were lying in the dark spent with their chests heaving once more.

Sometimes she'd wake him up with her mouth around his cock, sucking at him gently and slowly, until his tip would burst in an eruption of sweet salt, filling her mouth with his delicious seed.

She loved teasing him, just as much as he loved teasing her. Each session blurred into another, an orgasmic journey of bliss that never ended or began. Moments between being with Eric were simply brief reprieves from the never-ending torrent of their love. Each time they'd come back together with their hunger renewed.

Claire had anticipated that it was just puppy love, just some mild infatuation that would cease as their time together grew longer. She suspected the desire to have him constantly inside of her would subside. If anything, the desire only heightened, and she sensed it was the same with him too. Words soon became an encumbrance, and they communicated everything they had to say with their eyes. He would stare at her with lust-laden ferocity, his ruby-red eyes speaking orders to her.

Open your legs—or—lift your dress up—or—fuck me, now.

They developed a wordless language with each other, and they both seemed to understand it without difficulty.

Their time together was finally broken when Eric was called to the other side of the castle on family business. He had only been gone a few hours, but when he finally returned they were on each other like lovers that had been separated for months.

While Eric had been gone, Claire had put on a long floral dress and twisted her hair into braids. Upon his return, his eyes sparkled with need.

"Oh my goodness, Claire." Eric locked the bolt of his bedroom door and turned to face his lover. With three quick strides he was across the room with his arms around her, his lips crushing against hers, his tongue sliding into her mouth. Claire hummed in pleasure as he squeezed her in his hands, opening her legs and allowing her body to melt into his. She felt herself go wet instantly at his touch, her panties becoming soaked as he turned her around slowly.

"I missed you so much," she whispered in the dim room, placing her hands on the dresser.

His hands gathered gentle bunches of her dress and he pulled it up slowly. Her breath shuddered as she felt the hem trace over her knees and up the outside of her thigh, until he had lifted it over her hips. His palms smoothed up and down the outsides of her creamy thighs, then he turned them in and moved up the insides, until he was cupping the damp patch of fabric between her legs. He pressed gently, sinking a fingertip into the wide line of her cunt. A second later his thumbs were hooked into the waistband of her white cotton panties, rolling them down onto the floor, leaving them twisted around her knees. Then his hands were back at her pussy, kneading her button with one hand while the other traced delicate circles up and down her tight slit.

Claire's breath leapt from her mouth in a series of protracted groans, shaking and panting as his fingers made her cum once more. She came hard, bending down until she was over the dresser. Her pussy quivered in need, while her cream dripped from her lips and down the insides of her thighs. Eric gently pulsed two fingers in and out of her, drawing them up her line until he found her ass. She closed her eyes and gasped silently as he entered her there too.

She heard the sound of his other hand sliding up and down his shaft, spreading her juices over him. Her skin tingled with the strange yet familiar fire that now burned across it dimly on a daily basis. The heat had grown with each of their meetings, turning up its intensity at every encounter, always remaining in the background, becoming stronger and more irresistible every day, never receding, never cooling. She groaned as the dull ache whispered over her skin, her mind screaming for his cock to be inside of her pussy, her heart yearning to feel his juices spilling into the last part of her that was virgin to him.

Heat from the round tip of his erection flared against her ass as he pushed tightly against her. She smiled as she heard him breathing in excitement, his hands sinking into her flesh as he pushed inside of her.

"Yes baby..." she moaned to him. "Fill me again. Fuck me again. Take me master, take me."

Her words spurred him on, and she cried in pleasure as the thick oak of his cock buried all the way inside of her. She bobbed her hips back and forth with a teasing rhythm that was familiar to her now. He gave her a slight spank, gliding in and out of her with ease, his base thumping gently against her ass and throbbing pussy with each slow thrust.

THE VAMPIRE'S SLAVE

Within minutes their rhythm and pleasure had crested together once more. A babble of joyous groans leapt from Claire's lips as Eric rolled his hips in and out of her, squeezing his hands into her body as he fucked her from behind.

It was then that something new happened, something entirely unexpected. Three words leapt from Claire's mouth in the heat of the moment. She had no idea why she said them, but she said them nonetheless.

"I love you," she gasped. "I love you, Eric. I love you, I love you, I love you."

He didn't stop, and he didn't slow. There was only silence for a second, but to her it felt like a passing eternity. He replied instantly, his voice lined in the tone of proud possession.

"I love you too," he groaned, rolling his body against hers as they shared the moment for the first time. "Now and forever."

She dropped her head back, half turned and found his lips, crushing against them until she had no breath left to give. He came hard inside of her, holding himself tight against her as he erupted, his cock flooding her body with half a dozen strings of his thick and molten love.

The sensation spurred her fire to new heights, and Claire crowed her joy across the dark room as the orgasm took over her body. He held himself against her until he was done, their lips rolling together in a passion of fire and fury.

Finally, he pulled out of her, and they fell onto the bed in a breathless pile, his arms circled around her, protecting her, holding her, nourishing her.

It took energy from Claire being with Eric, and it had taken her some time to tolerate the extreme physical demand that being with a vampire required. As they lay there panting in the dark, she held her heavy eyes open for as long as possible, staring at her lover beneath the lids of her lust-filled eyes.

"It's burning now," she said. "More than ever. I tried to keep the fire down, but I can't keep it down anymore. When I wake I'll need you. I'm ready for you, Eric. I'm ready."

She saw a spark in his eyes, a spark that sang acknowledgment and eager curiosity.

"I could sense it in you," he said calmly. "I've been able to sense it for some time now. When you wake you'll be in a frenzy, and there will be nothing you can do to stop yourself. There's not much sense in asking. You will be in control when you wake."

Claire laughed to herself as she felt the heavy sleep tugging at the last strings of her consciousness. "I thought you were the one in control? I thought I was merely the vessel that contained your lust?"

"We're both in control." He smiled, kissed her, and twisted her lower lip gently between his teeth while his palms squeezed a handful of her ass. "But when you wake it will be completely different. Rest now, for you will need it. When you wake the burning will be unbearable, but fear not, for I will be there to answer the cry of your desire."

"You promise?" Heat flared across her skin and Claire let out a cry of pain, feeling the last waking sensation of her full frenzy.

"I promise," he said. "I promise."

CHAPTER TEN

Eric

ERIC WOKE IN THE NIGHT TO AN INTENSE HEAT, burning through his veins like hellfire.

Jesus. What is this?!

He stood from the bed, staring down at his arms in the dark of the room. All of his senses seemed to burn through him, picking up every perceptible detail. He felt his blood swimming through his veins, coursing through his muscles. His eyes strained and he saw beads of sweat forming on the tiny ridges of his fingertips. His head waned and twisted with a strange spinning heat. He clutched at his temples with his fingertips, screaming through the pain. Up until now, he had forgotten where he was, who he was, who he was with. It came back to him, and he spun back to the bed, his pupils like pinpricks.

"Claire? Where are you?! Claire!"

The bed was empty, and there was no sign of Claire in the room. Sound flooded back into Eric's ears, and the temporary flare of his mating fever seemed to subside. His senses drew back, and his eyesight returned to the enhanced form of vision that was normal for him. The world hissed against his eardrums until he was hearing regularly once more. He heard his own breath racing in the dark of the room. It was raining outside. A crack of thunder illuminated the valley beneath his window, casting a brief flash of white across the room. Eric saw the shadow on the wall in front of him, and he turned to the window to face his visitor.

"Ira? Is that you?"

The Victorian-clad doctor stepped forward from the shadows, his face illuminated by a pale ray of moonlight. A dark smiled tugged at the corner of his thin lips. The shadows beneath his hollow eyes twitched, a flicker of amusement passing over his face.

"Where is Claire?!" Eric shouted. "What is happening?"

"I'm afraid your darling mate has been taken from you, Eric."

A beat of dread passed through Eric's body; he caught his breath and tightened his fists.

"Explain yourself," he growled. "What have you done with her?"

"It's not so much what I've done with her," Ira smiled. "It's what I'm going to do."

Eric cast his eyes around the room quickly, trying to get a bearing of his surroundings. Ira had been in the room and he hadn't noticed, but that was because his senses had been impaired by his mating frenzy.

Take a deep breath and scan the room, he reminded himself.

Eric strained his ears to hear the presence of any other creature within the radius of his room. He heard the heartbeat of another, and he recognized it instantly.

"Ezra?" He said her name out loud, half confused.

"Oh you always were the smartest one, Eric. Come out, Ezra."

A dim humming noise filled the room and the lights overhead turned on one by one, illuminating the darkness. Eric turned around to see Ezra gliding through the door, her eyes rolled over white. Eric realized instantly that Ezra wasn't in control of herself; she was possessed.

"What have you done to her?" Eric hissed, spinning back to face Ira. "How are you doing this?"

"I've spent so many years reading, watching, waiting. Moving between the great families as an archivist, a researcher, a doctor. You were all very keen to use the resource that was my knowledge, but you never really considered me one of you. None of you did."

"You're wrong," Eric spat. "You've been considered a member of this family for as long as I remember."

"Exactly," Ira spat. "And that was the problem. Ira of the Vandark, Ira of the Caravo, Ira of the Belmont. Everywhere I went I was an asset, I was a tool. One thousand years of servitude and not once was I offered my own seat, my own castle."

"Is that what this all about?" Eric laughed. "You want a castle of your own where you can hang a crest on the wall? Parade around servants of your own?"

Ira's faced twitched momentarily at Eric's mocking.

"No. I want more than that, and I've been waiting for my chance to seize it. I don't want a mere castle, I want the whole world. I will take control of our world. I will be a ruler of all vampires."

"You're a crazy bastard," Eric hissed, "and my family will murder you before we let you attempt such a thing."

"You can try," Ira laughed, pacing back and forth across the room, an air of control dominating his every movement. "But you might struggle. I have control of Ezra and her faculties. I have control of others within the castle too. I have chosen only the strong. I have been building the strength to use this incantation for years. Now that it's working, nothing can stop me."

"Playing around with magic? A dangerous thing, Ira. You will be your own undoing, I guarantee it."

"I highly doubt that, Belmont. Anyway, come...I tire of talking to you of my plan. Come with me and I will put it into fruition before your very eyes."

"What are you talking about?" Eric hissed. "Tell me what you've done with Claire or I'll kill you."

Eric jumped at Ira with his arms out, ready to grab the doctor by the neck and break it clean in two. He'd barely moved from the floor when Ira waved a hand in Ezra's direction. Eric's body froze in midair and he felt himself suspended in a wave of ice-cold fire. He strained to turn his head, and saw Ezra holding her hand out toward him. He looked back to Ira and realized what was happening. Ira was using Ezra to control the inhabitants of the castle.

"You bastard. You're not going to get away with this."

"Of course I am. I've been planning it for a hundred years. All I was waiting for was a breeder, and you got her nice and ready for me. Come, let's go up to the roof. You can watch me rape your stupid little whore, just before I throw you and your family into the river below."

*

Using Ezra's power, Ira dragged Eric through the hallways of the castle. Eric twisted in the air the whole while, fighting against the hijacked witch's power. He knew that struggling was no use, and that Ezra's hold over him would be too strong, but he fought nonetheless. They walked up the center spiral of the castle, the main pathway that led up to the roof.

"Where are we going? Why up here?"

"After I use your whore in front of you and send your family into the river below, I'll be leaving this hellhole," Ira chuckled, walking a few steps ahead of Eric's position. Ezra walked at the back of the pack, her hands extended outward, keeping Eric frozen.

"There's a reason for this storm."

Wind battered at the walls of the spire outside, while thunder rolled through the air all around them. Eric glanced left out a narrow window in high spire, and caught glimpse of the storm that raged outside.

"It's all part of the incantation," Ira explained. "I've been summoning the energy to do this for months. Harnessing the power of the storm, I could take control of the witch, the golems within the castle, and I even had energy left over to open a portal."

"A portal?" Eric tried not to betray his surprise. Portals were a rare feat of magic, and only the most accomplished sorcerers could summon them.

Ira turned back to face Eric. "Yes, you don't think I'd start my dynasty here do you?" He laughed. "You vampires have such a penchant for the macabre. I will build a real fortress. It will make this wreck of a castle look like a stone shack."

They came to the top of the spiral staircase and walked through an open door that led onto the broad rooftop of the Castle Belmont. Eric caught sight of the gruesome scene Ira had orchestrated, and felt fury instantly burning within him.

Ira had positioned five stakes against the northeast corner. The stakes were set into the stone wall, angled back so they hovered over the river far below. On four of the five stakes were the remaining members of his family. His father, Wraith, Veronica, and Sophia.

Just away from the stakes, a table had been positioned, on which Ira had tied Claire. Eric felt his whole body burning with fury to free the girl, and he also felt the burning heat of his mating frenzy too.

Finally, set into a wall just left of the table, a portal sat burning through stone, giving brief glimpses of some far and distant room. All the while the storm raged around them, wind and rain whipped across the broad stone expanse, biting at Eric's skin from every angle. The wind screeched all around them, and thunder rumbled through the valley several times a minute. The scene was illuminated by the high torches that covered the walls of the Castle Belmont, and white sheets of lightning added to the chaos.

"The last stake is for you. Ezra. Do the honors."

Eric growled as the witch moved his body swiftly through the air, fastening it to the last stake with magic bindings. He cast a quick glance over his shoulder into the valley below, where the river swam deep below them.

His stake was the last in the row. Beside him was his youngest sister Sophia, Wraith, Veronica, and then his father. Sophia cried in fear upon seeing her brother being tied next to her.

"Eric, please! Do something!"

"It's all right, Sophia. I'll get us out of this, I promise!"

Eric heard Ira laughing somewhere ahead. He looked over and saw the doctor fiddling with a mountain of luggage that had been arranged by the portal. Stone golems were carrying more boxes out by the minute. Eric looked across at his family. Sophia was the only one looking back at him. Veronica and his father had their eyes trained keenly on Ira, their faces etched with a fury that Eric supposed was similar to his own. Wraith's eyes had rolled over white and his face was cast up to the sky. Eric heard Claire's voice, and his eyes were on her in an instant.

"Eric? Eric is that you? Please help me! It burns so much, it burns so!"

"Claire! What did he do to you?! I'll save us, I promise. Just hang in there!"

Claire was tied to the table in the pajamas she had fallen asleep in. Her eyes were blindfolded. She flinched at the sound of Eric's voice. Eric turned his attention on Ira.

"What have you done to her, you sick bastard?"

Ira spun from his trove of pillaged treasure, seeming to remember he had prisoners at his command.

"I haven't done anything, you stupid fool!"

He walked back from the portal, past the table and paraded in front of the family. "You really think I'd risk hurting a breeder? She's burning because of her mating frenzy! Her body is craving sex. No worry, for I shall give it to her now. And then I will force stakes into your hearts and cast you into the river."

"No, please!" Sophia cried out at Ira's threat. Ira simply cackled in response. Eric looked at his sister, who was trembling in terror.

Another voice came from the other end of the line. Eric glanced sideways to see it was his oldest sister, Veronica. Her eyes burned into Ira's while the wind dragged her red hair across her pale face.

"You don't have to kill us, Ira. Take the girl if you must, but let us live. There's no sense in this."

Ira smirked and walked up to Veronica, stopping just in front of her stake. "You really think I'm that stupid? You would come after me as soon as you could. I've been the subject of your bastard father long enough to know that truth." Ira looked at Atticus, who simply stared back.

"What? No words for me, old man?"

"If you're going to do it then just do it," Atticus growled. "You always did take too fucking long with everything."

As Eric watched the exchange between his family and his captor, he looked at his brother Wraith, who seemed far removed from the scene before them. His face was twisted up at the sky, his eyes filled with white. Eric could see the reflection of the storm in his brother's blank stare. The faint trace of a smile hung on Wraith's lips. The expression felt familiar to Eric, for he felt he had seen this look on his brother once before. The night that Wraith's body had been taken prisoner and possessed by the demon.

"What have you done to Wraith?" Eric shouted over the commotion of the storm as he watched Ira approach the table upon which Claire was restrained. He trembled in rage as he watched Ira draw a hand up the inside of Claire's thigh. He broke away for a moment to answer Eric's question.

"That fool? Nothing. His mind is so weak, it seems to have been possessed as a side effect. Another testament to the weakness of the Belmont lineage."

Ira's hands were back on Claire again, but for a moment, Eric saw past the transgression. If Ira didn't have control of Wraith, then that meant his brother still had control of himself. Ira didn't know the Belmont family secret. He didn't know the truth about Wraith. That meant there might still be a chance.

"Eric is that you?" Claire writhed on the table underneath Ira's touch, her arms and legs struggling at the bindings. "I've been waiting for your touch for so long. Please take me!"

"Yes, it's me, darling," Ira said, taking advantage of Claire in the confusion of her sexual frenzy. "You want me to mate you darling, don't you? You want me to fuck your cunt with my dick?"

"Stop that, you bastard! She doesn't know what she's saying! This isn't fair!" Eric lunged against the restraints, trying to break the magic that held him to the stake, knowing that it was impossible. His father spoke from the end of the line.

"You'll kill her, Ira. You know that. Her body is only suited for Eric. You'll only end up killing her."

"Probably," Ira laughed. "But what's the harm in trying? She's deep in the heat of her frenzy. She won't know the difference..."

Ira pulled back the blindfold that was on Claire's face, allowing her to see the scene around her for the first time.

"You want me inside you, don't you, Claire? You want to be my slave for all time."

Eric could hear Ira trying to flare his intention, which in comparison to his own was weak and pathetic. Claire's face twisted in confusion at the sound of Ira's weedy voice.

"Eric? Eric... that isn't Eric."

Her eyes widened in realization that it wasn't her lover hovering over her. "You? You?! No! Get away from me! Don't touch me! Eric, Eric, help me!"

Ira's cool resolve melted for the first time, replaced by incarnate rage. Eric smiled weakly at the sight. "It's okay, darling. I'll save you, I promise."

"It doesn't matter if she wants me or not," Ira said with a tone of finality. "I'll make her mine either way, and place my child in her womb. I'll lock her in the tower of my new fortress, and keep her there for all time, using her over and over until I have an army big enough to take over the world!"

Ira wrapped his hands around the waistband of Claire's pajama trousers and yanked them down, stripping her lower half in one powerful move.

"There's just one small problem with your plan, Ira."

The doctor looked up from Claire one last time to meet Eric's sneering expression.

"Oh yeah? And what's that?"

"You forgot about my brother."

Eric turned to the vacant expression of his brother, and he stirred every ounce of his Intention. He called to him, pushing his voice deep into the mind of the vessel that was once his twin. He found the demon that had lain dormant within him all these years, finally woken by the storm tonight.

"Wraith! Look at me, it's your brother, Eric!"

Eric howled over the orchestra of the storm. Wraith turned to him, his white eyes reflecting the chaos of the night overhead. He spoke to Eric with a voice that the family hadn't heard for a long time. It wasn't the hollow voice of the demon that possessed him; it was his voice, soft, frightened—the voice of someone that had been trapped by a demon for a lifetime.

"Eric? Eric is that you? It's been such a long time, brother."

"Stop this!" Ira yelled, clearly perturbed by the eerie scene unfolding between Eric and Wraith. "Stop this nonsense at once! You won't stop me from taking your stupid human!"

Eric ignored Ira's attempt to distract him. He knew he only had a brief chance to hold Wraith's attention. "Wraith! I need you to do me a favor, I need you to take hold of the demon within you and use it to attack Ezra, can you do that?"

Wraith's white eyes glanced at the drop below him.

"But the fall..."

"If you don't do this we'll all die, Wraith, you included!"

The white eyes of his brother passed over the scene in front of him, as if seeing it for the first time. He took it all in, considered something for a moment, and then he nodded solemnly.

"Stop this now!" Ira screamed, climbing from the table to confront the brothers. He turned to Ezra and held a hand in her direction. "Witch, I've had enough, kill the brothers first!"

Eric turned to his brother, who was staring back at him with all his focus. Wraith spoke, his own voice entwined with the spirit of the demon possessing him.

"Now?"

"Now!" Eric screamed back. "Attack!"

*

The storm swelled in the sky above, and in an instant, war broke out on the rooftop of the Castle Belmont. Ira left Claire on the table to deal with Eric and Wraith. He stood, body shaking, a hand stretched in Ezra's direction, hoping that the witch would carry out his order in time.

"Kill them!" he screamed. "Kill them both!"

His order came at the same time as Eric's. The possessed hands of the witch flew up and red light frothed at her fingertips, but all eyes were on Wraith.

The brother raised his eyes to the sky, and a horrific groan left from the tortured creature's lips as if he were letting out a great torrent of energy. Suddenly, the thunder and lightning in the sky above intensified tenfold, and a bolt of white electricity thundered down through the night, right into the body of Wraith.

The fire of a thousand suns coursed through the body of Wraith, and the electricity swam through his veins, breaking the magical shackles set on him by Ezra. Lightning channeled down through his body, Wraith lifted his arms and pointed them at Ezra, pushing the raw energy of the storm out through his palms.

A colossal trail of white light leapt from Wraith's hands, his throat screaming a hoarse cry of pain all the while. The bolt leapt straight through the air into Ezra. The witch was sent flying back across the rooftop, crashing into a distant wall. Ira's dark possession of her broke immediately, for each one of the Belmont family fell forward from their stakes and dropped to the ground, their magical shackles existing no more.

Eric jumped to his feet and set his eyes on Ira. The doctor was already making a run for the portal, realizing that his plan had failed.

"Not a chance," Eric growled as he leapt through the air, and in one swift movement he was across the roof and his hands were around the neck of the treacherous doctor. Ira looked up at Eric in horror, his face burning with fear.

"Eric, no! Please! It's all a big misunder—"

Eric shot his hands to one side, immediately breaking the neck of the doctor. He left him standing for a moment and a fraction of a second later he was back in front of the traitor holding a stake. He plunged the wood through his chest without saying a word, and turned without stopping to watch him burst into dust.

A moment later he was at Claire's side, untying her from the bench with the help of his sister Sophia. As soon as she was free, they helped her redress. Eric picked Claire up from the table and held her in his arms, squeezing her as tight as he could.

"Eric! Eric is that you?!"

"I'm sorry." He repeated the words a thousand times over. "I should never have let this happen, I'm so sorry."

She squeezed him back even harder.

"Don't be stupid. This isn't your fault. Can you set me down?"

"Oh no." Eric shook his head. "I'm never letting go of you again. Seems every time I do something bad happens."

"She'll be all right now."

Eric turned at the sound of Veronica's voice.

"You must be Claire, I'm Veronica. Eric's older sister."

Eric begrudgingly set Claire down. She brushed herself off momentarily and took the hand of the redhaired girl.

"Hell of a way to meet each other."

"Well, I wish the circumstances could have been better, but yes. It's nice to finally meet the latest addition to our family."

Atticus and Sophia stopped at the side of Veronica, and the family stood as a unit, staring around them at the aftermath of chaos that Ira had left.

Eric's eyes darted around the roof, surveying the damage. The portal through which Ira had tried to escape still whirled on the wall. The golem Ira had possessed had turned back into inanimate statues, frozen in time until magic would wake them again.

"Wraith!"

Eric turned in the direction of the stakes upon which he and his family had been tied. He walked toward them quickly, pulling Claire by the hand as he did so.

"Four," he said quietly to himself, realizing there was one stake missing. His father spoke from behind him.

"The stake he was tied to fell when the lightning struck. The blast must have been too much."

Eric looked over the edge of the castle wall where the stake had been fixed into the stone. The river raged peacefully hundreds of feet beneath them.

"We can still save him!" Sophia said hopefully. "We can send a party to look for him!"

Eric turned and saw Veronica and Sophia staring at his father with the same hopeful expression.

"No," Atticus said gravely. "The blast, the fall—there's not a chance he survived."

"He gave his life to save us." Sophia started to weep, throwing herself into the chest of her father.

"Did it leave him?" Veronica said, looking at her father.

"The demon? I can't say for sure. All I know is that he saved us all. I hope he found peace in his last moments."

Eric turned around to look back at that fall below. His eyes wandered over the dark landscape, knowing full well that his brother was dead. Claire's hand tightened around his own. He looked at her and smiled softly.

"He saved us all," she said. "He was a hero."

"Indeed," Eric said sadly. He knew that for the majority of his life, his brother had been haunted by the demon inside of him. He hoped, as his father did, that there had been peace somewhere in his final moments.

"Stop, witch!" Everyone spun on their feet at Veronica's voice. Ezra stumbled toward them, tendrils of smoke rising from her body. Atticus put a hand out in front of his daughter, who was ready to launch into battle.

"At ease, Veronica," Atticus said. "I think we have our old Ezra back. Is that right?"

Everyone looked at Ezra, who had been on the receiving end of a bolt of lightning. Her hair was a mass of black wire, her clothes were ripped and smoking. Her skin was marred with dark smoking burns, her eyes scored with red. She spoke, her voice etched with the pain of suffering.

"You are right, Atticus, you old fool."

Everyone took a deep breath and relaxed at hearing Ezra's usual voice. She looked at the aftermath for the first time, taking it all in with jaded realization.

"Ira. What a cunning bastard. I should have known he was up to something. He's been sneaking around my library for months. I didn't think the bastard had it in him."

"None of us did," Atticus said. "Are you all right?"

"I'm okay. That was an old incantation he used to take over my body. I should have seen it coming. This is my fault."

"None of this is anyone's fault," Eric said. "We couldn't have known Ira would betray us like this, after all these years."

Ezra turned to the portal and held out her hands. "I'd better close this."

"Wait a moment." Eric walked back to the group to get a better look at the portal. He kept a tight hold on Claire. "It's just as I thought. Father, Veronica—look through the portal. Do you see anything that looks familiar?"

They looked through the portal. On the other side there was a stone room of some sort, in a keep in some unknown location. Boxes of luggage and pillaged artifacts lay in the room, along with the frozen stone giants that Ira had cursed to do his bidding.

"On the far wall." Veronica lifted a hand and pointed through the portal.

"The sign of the White Order," Atticus said. "We should close this portal at once."

"What about the things?" Sophia said. "There are several artifacts I can see from here that belong to our family."

"That is a room in the fortress of the White Order," Atticus said calmly. "There's no telling what spells they have in place to protect themselves against vampires."

"But Ira—"

"Was obviously working alongside them. I dare say he had some form of protection. It's not worth the risk. They're just things. I've already lost one child today, I will not lose another."

Atticus turned from Sophia to Ezra and they nodded. Ezra flared her fingers and the portal was closed a moment later. She turned to the stakes which had been on the wall. "So Wraith is dead? I can't say I'm surprised. That bolt he hit me with was stronger than anything I've ever felt before. It must have tore his body apart leaving the demon like that."

Eric looked at Ezra. "You knew he was possessed? But how? Only the family knew."

"The demon that was inside your brother was well hidden, I'll admit. But such things are easy for a witch to spot."

"You knew and you didn't help him?" Veronica clenched her fists, anger and sadness swirling in her blood-red eyes.

"There was nothing I could do to help him, child. The demon that had taken residence in your brother is stronger than anything I've ever seen before. I'm surprised he lived as long as he did. He was strong."

The group fell into reflective silence, looking over the smoking wreckage left from the battle.

"Wraith died a long time ago," Eric said mournfully. "I haven't known my brother in a long time. His death was not in vain. May the earth have mercy on his soul."

The family stood in somber reflection, nodding at Eric's words.

Finally Atticus spoke.

"We will properly honor Wraith's sacrifice soon. But first we need to rebuild. We should probably all get to cleaning things up. Ezra, perform a perimeter check of the castle. It's likely that Ira was working alone, but I want to be sure."

Ezra nodded. "Of course."

"And I will come too," Veronica said.

"Of course. Make sure you see Sophia to her room safely first. And Eric..."

Eric turned to the voice of his father.

"See to it that you get Claire back to your room safe. We shall reconvene soon to plan our next move as a family from here."

"Yes, Father."

With that the group broke off into parts. Ezra woke the golems that Ira had taken control of, setting them to work on cleaning up the mess the battle had left behind. Eric walked Claire to the southwest corner of the roof.

"Where are we going?" Claire asked as she followed him.

"I thought we could use the entrance at the southwest corner. The main staircase at the center will be full of golem, and I don't fancy squeezing around them in a tight space."

Claire stopped to look at a purple blemish far on the horizon.

"Dawn is breaking," she said with some trepidation.

"Not to fear," Eric smiled. "There's still an hour or so until the light will touch the castle. Do you remember the first time I brought you to the castle? This is were we first landed."

Claire smiled fondly in remembrance for something that had been a true nightmare at the time.

"I do remember," she smiled. "I was nearly frozen half to death because you carried me here naked."

Eric took Claire in his arms and they laughed together, watching the sunrise in the distance.

"I know. I was foolish back then. I feel as if I'm a completely different person now."

"Me too," Claire said, turning in his arms to face him. They kissed briefly, holding one another as the rest of the world melted away. "My fever still burns. But it seems to have cooled a little."

"Of course," Eric said. "It must have been hell for you tied to that table. It will come back again, you realize. I guarantee I will be ready for you this time."

Claire placed a hand on Eric's chest and looked into his eyes. "I already feel it coming back."

Eric grabbed her hand and placed his forehead against hers, looking deep into her eyes. "Why don't we go back to the room? We can forget about all this for now. Let's just make it about me and you again, as it should be."

"That sounds nice, but I was wondering if you could do something for me first."

"Anything," Eric said, squeezing her hand. "What is it?"

Claire turned out to the distant sunset, looking down at the land beneath the castle. "Let me fly with you again. Carry me through the air one more time."

She turned back to Eric to see the blood red in his eyes twinkling with mischief. He scooped her up in his arms and a second later he was standing on the edge of the castle wall, holding Claire over the dizzying fall below. Claire let out a shriek and laughed, half-panicked.

"Eric, be careful!" She wrapped her arms tightly around her man as she looked down at the distant earth below.

"No worries, my darling." Eric crouched down for a moment and stood up tall, a thundering groan leaping from his throat as he stretched out his wings. "No harm will come to you anymore. I swear that with my life."

Eric tightened his hold on Claire and fell forward over the edge. They fell through the air, hurtling toward the earth, Claire screaming all the while. He gathered air beneath his wings and waited until the last possible moment. The tips of the forest below them were inches from his face when he spread his wings properly, launching them back up into the air, speeding like a dark bullet into the night.

CHAPTER ELEVEN

Claire

IT WAS THE SECOND TIME CLAIRE HAD FLOWN with Eric, but the circumstances this time were significantly different. He carried her through the air and around the grounds of the castle, twisting and turning through the air like an ivory arrow. Claire kept tight hold of him all the while, safe in the comfort of his embrace. It was one thing to see the castle from the highest point, but it was another altogether to see it from the air.

They looped around the castle, through the grounds and the surrounding landscape several times, and Claire gained a new appreciation for the beauty of the castle and its scenery. The sun rose in the distance, bruising the black ink of the sky with deep blotches of purple, which were slowly turning into lighter shades of blue and violet. Eric finally pulled back as the morning dawned upon the valley, with the promise to take Claire into the sky whenever she liked.

By the time they got back to his room on the southwest corner of the ninth floor, the altercation with Ira almost felt like a distant nightmare. Eric held Claire in his arms until the very last moment, only setting her down once the bedroom door was closed and locked behind him.

After he laid her down on the floor, she kissed him and thanked him promptly, staring in amazement at the blank space on his back where his wings had been just only moments before. She felt herself marveling at his beauty as she always did, but she felt something else stirring within her now, a great fondness that was burning inside her, brighter than it ever had before.

"It won't be long until the frenzy takes us both again." Eric brushed aside a wayward lock of Claire's wind-strewn hair. "We should probably rest before then."

"Actually..." Claire took his hand in hers and let her eyes drop down to the ground. "I was wondering if we could go back to your other bedroom. The one we were in originally?"

Claire looked around the room where she and Eric had spent much of their time together in the last week, exploring one another's bodies to the fullest extent. She liked this room, it was modern and clean, but it lacked the authenticity of Eric's other room. She knew the other place was *his* and was a true representation of who he was.

"But the bathroom—"

"I'm sure it's been cleaned by now." Claire waved a hand at the notion. She had been bothered by it once upon a time, the place where Wraith's demon had left the bodies. But it didn't bother her anymore.

"I've seen enough in these last weeks not to trivialize something like *that* Eric. But I can't let it control me forever. I want to go back to the room that is yours. If you're going to take my body, then I want it to be there."

His eyes widened at her words, and his lips twitched.

"Very well. Come, we will waste no further time."

His hand wrapped around hers and they left the room, trudging back through the corridors back to room on the northeast corner. His very touch breathed electricity through her body, and the slightest sensation made her body wild with desire. She could sense that the frenzy was returning, the heat was stirring up in her once again, but it was coming faster this time.

As they walked all external stimuli seemed to strip away. It was as if her mind was only prepared to focus its energy on one thing: Eric and Eric alone. Her vision went black around the edges, until the only thing she could see was Eric, a solitary point of alabaster perfection leading her through the darkness to her much sought-after destination. Her hearing faded out until she could only hear his voice and his footsteps, along with the rhythmic throbbing of her heart. The air was laced with the scent of his body, so close and so potent it was almost as if she could taste the sweet sweat on his skin. His hand held hers gently, and she felt every ridge of his fingertips, pressing smoothly into her palm.

The sound of a door opening came from somewhere in the distant black and then it shut again. He turned to her, meeting her gaze with his twinkling ruby eyes, his voice trickling over her like liquid velvet.

"This is it. Are you ready?"

She nodded, her lips open in expectation, her throat unable to give words any longer. This was it, it was finally happening.

She was about to become his.

*

Their lips crashed together, slow and sensual at first, then fast and furious, like a rapid torrent.

His lips moved to her throat, sucking at her sweet and pale flesh with fervor. Claire dropped her head back, moaned and pulled herself closer against him.

"Oh Eric..." His hands moved deftly across the buttons on her shirt. His thumbs moved over her breasts softly, running small circles over the delicate points. She threaded her fingers through the dark weave of his hair, holding him close against her as his lips worked down her neck to the top of her chest. He finished unbuttoning her shirt and pulled back the fabric, revealing the milky-white flesh of her torso. Claire helped him, pulling her arms free of the fabric, letting the shirt slip backward off her hands and onto the floor. She worked at her bra quickly, sliding it off too, baring herself to him.

His twinkling red eyes darted up and down her body as he stood with his arms around her hips. "Good Lord you are beautiful beyond words." He crouched, bringing his lips against her breasts, sucking at her nipples. His hands smoothed down the curve of her back to her front, his fingers like ice on her skin.

"You feel so good..." she whispered into his ear. He wrapped his hands around the bottom of his gray shirt and pulled it up and off his head, letting it drop to the floor. The muscular splendor of his torso was hers alone now, to watch and worship as much as she wanted. Claire ran her hands over his body greedily as their lips came together, marveling at the solid warmth of his muscle. His arms moved around her again and tugged her waist against his, crushing their torsos together softly. The soft firmness of her breasts squished against the hardness of his chest and abs. Claire ran her hands down the sides of his muscular torso, tracing the belt of muscle down until she reached the crotch of his jeans.

"Let's not forget this either..." She fumbled with them for a second, before pulling them open and shimmying them down his legs. He helped her, stepping out of the jeans and leaving them behind on the floor. They stood before each other now in just underwear and then, as if they read each other's minds, they stripped simultaneously. Their bodies came together once more, completely naked this time.

Claire moaned as their lips entwined. His hands wrapped around the full flesh of her buttocks, squeezing tight and pulling her hips against his. Her pussy tingled with warmth, and she felt herself becoming slick with unbearable excitement. The hard line of his cock pressed against her tummy, branding it like a red-hot iron. His lips pulled away from hers and whispered into her ear.

"On the bed. Now."

His voice was more of a growl than anything, and it sent a warm shiver down her spine. Claire was ready to run to the bed, but Eric threw his hands around her waist and pulled her up, forcing her to wrap her legs around him. She felt the hard ridges of his muscled abs pressing against her wet cunt, deliciously rubbing against her with each step he took.

He threw her down onto the bed, and before she could realize what was happening, he was on top of her, his lips worshiping her body once more. His hand slipped up between her thighs, his fingers brushing over the delicate softness of her flesh. His fingers found her clit, wet and throbbing, and he pushed against her delicately, rubbing gentle circles.

Claire let out a sharp moan and pulled her legs apart, pushing her hips up so his erection was pressing against her open pussy like a raw brand.

"I can't wait anymore, Eric. Take me. Take me now!"

She felt the heat of the frenzy dancing over her body like a thousand points of flame. She looked at Eric and she knew he felt the same. The blood-red sparkle of his eyes had been lost to two giant pools of black, and his teeth had twisted into two sharp points of white against his ruby-red lips.

"Mate me, Eric." She pushed her lips against his, flicking her tongue over the points of his teeth. Her hand moved down the broad muscle of his back, down to the firm curve of his near-perfect ass. She gripped him tight and squeezed, pulling him against her.

Somehow, his cock seemed to swell even further in size. Claire let out a gasp as she felt his raging affection press against the top of her crotch. She looked down at him and felt her eyes bulge in response.

"You're huge," she said, doe-eyed. "You've grown." Eric had his hand around the thick base of his cock, which hadn't only grown in length but in girth as well. It was no secret that Eric had a huge cock. They had done plenty of anal together in preparation for their mating and Claire had almost grown used to his huge size. This however...

"I did tell you..." He pushed the thick and bulbous head of his shaft between the glistening folds of her pussy and pressed forward gently. Claire's whole body rocked in response and she felt her pussy clenching in anticipation. This was the moment she had been waiting for, this was the thing she had wanted since she had first laid eyes on him in the corridor. "We vampires are different."

He inched his hips forward, and her pussy spread around him, opening wider as his cock slipped inside of her. Claire gasped and wrapped her hands around him tightly as he worked his way inside. He filled her like a warm pillar of steel, and her whole body shivered in delight.

Slowly but surely, he disappeared inside of her inch by inch, until the thick base of his cock came up against the bottom of her pussy. They were both lost in the throes of passion now, the black expanses of their eyes lost in one another's gaze. Eric rolled his hips back, drawing his cock out of her almost all the way, then he pushed back in, penetrating her properly for the first time.

She let out a large moan, half smiling and half laughing in joy as he spread her love in two. She wrapped her hands around the broad muscles of his neck and pulled him down, their lips meeting once more as he started to pulse his cock in and out of her.

"Oh Eric... Eric it's so good!"

She spoke with long and protracted moans, little bubbles of joy escaping her lips as his thrusts came stronger and faster. Claire opened up her legs further, pushing her hips up to meet him, spreading herself as much as she possibly could.

His strong hands were on her legs, pushing them back until her feet were by her ears. She had relaxed fully, and he moved in and out of her easily now, the sound of her wetness clapping throughout the room.

The first orgasm came and it came hard, causing her lungs to belt out a long line of moans, as she scrunched her eyes tight, pulling the fabric on the bed. He came in her pussy for the first time, his cock erupted inside of her, pulsing thick jets of his love up and against her pink walls until she was covered completely.

Before she could process what was happening, he had her on her knees and he was behind her, his cock slipping inside of her cunt once more, his hips rolling back and forward wildly.

"Eric, Eric!" Claire grabbed her breasts and moaned his name in delight, while he fucked her hard from behind. His hands spanked her ass, traced up the curve of her hips, and squeezed into her waist as he thundered in and out of her. Her pussy throbbed and tingled in delight, and she came again several times, until her body was shaking and rasping, until her breath would come no longer.

Eric came over and over again, filling her pussy with mammoth waves of his love each time, until she could swear he would have nothing left to give. It kept coming though, and each time she felt it he grew harder, and each time she felt it he grew longer. His speed and fury increased, bringing her pleasure to its absolute zenith. Claire turned back and he moved so fast he appeared in a half-blur to her, the red-black of his eyes fixed on her own all the while.

He flipped onto his back and she climbed on top of him, squatting down onto his cock gingerly, only to be held there a few seconds later with his powerful hands on her waist as his girth hammered into her from below. His hands where everywhere at once, and they were everywhere when she wanted them to be. The huge cups of his palms smoothed over her breasts, the thick branches of his fingers brushed down over her hips.

She liked it most of all when he held his hands in the crease of her thigh and thrust up into her. She let her head fall back while her hands traced over her breasts, letting herself bounce on top of him as he filled her over and over.

Time became nothing, and the world shrank to the two of them. By the time they were done, Claire wasn't sure if hours or days had passed. All she knew was that he had brought her pleasure so vast and intense, that she had never known anything like it before.

After, they lay in the dim light of the room together for what felt like hours more, and he drew the tips of his fingers up and down her body, tracing every curve and every line. They fell into a deep sleep together, and when they woke they were on each other once more, his body answering every call of her mind.

They went like that for an eternity, only stopping to eat or sleep or bathe, most of the time disturbing these activities with the uncontrollable lust they felt for each other.

Eventually they finally felt the fever subsiding, and the itching heat that prickled through both of their bodies faded away, until the world came back into focus a little. Their libidos returned to a more normal level, albeit still far above normal.

After having her pussy fucked by his tongue in the shower, Claire dried herself off at her dresser, watching Eric as he wrapped the firm muscles of his torso in the coal–black shirt and jeans that fit him so well. She smiled at him and placed a hand over her stomach, looking down and wondering, hoping, that maybe she might be carrying a child of his.

Claire looked up into the mirror once more and was startled to see Eric standing behind her. He wrapped his arms around her and kissed her. She dropped her head back against his chest and sighed in contentment.

"You're wondering if you're pregnant," he said with a soft smile.

"I thought you weren't reading my mind anymore."

"Again. I don't have to read your mind to know what you're thinking."

"When will I know?" she asked, turning to face him as he sat on the bed. Their hands twined together as they faced each other. "How will we know? We don't just do a test, do we?"

"We'll know soon," he said. "Trust me."

Claire looked down at the floor then back at Eric. "I'm worried that you got it wrong somehow, and that I'm not what you thought I was."

There was silence between them for a moment as he listened to her.

"What if I'm not a breeder?" Claire asked. "What if I'm just a regular human? Then all this was for nothing."

"Even if that were the case, I'd still love you until the day I die."

She tried to find the right words, and realized there was only one thing she really wanted to say. "I love you too."

Her heart fluttered in her chest a million miles an hour. Eric knelt forward and kissed her. His lips lingered on hers, and her heart swelled with happiness.

"*Even* if that were the case," Eric repeated. "Which it's not. You are *definitely* a breeder, my darling Claire. You smell much too delicious to be a regular human."

"You promise?"

"Yes, and whatever happens I love you either way."

"I love you too," she said. "I love you too."

EPILOGUE

Three months later.

"SO YOU'RE PROBABLY ALL WONDERING why we gathered you here." Claire stood next to Eric, and they shared a passing glance before looking back at the family sitting around them.

"I *certainly* am," Veronica quipped. "I'm supposed to be going out hunting. Come on already!"

"Simmer down, Veronica." Atticus flicked his eyes at his daughter. "Continue, Claire."

"Well," Claire took a deep breath and felt Eric's hand tighten around her own. "Eric and I have known for some time, but we wanted to keep it a secret for a while just to be sure—"

Before Claire could finish the rest of her sentence, Sophia pushed her chair back from the table. "No..." Her arms were locked out straight and her expression was frozen in anticipation.

"Yes..." Claire continued. "I'm pregnant. Eric and I are expecting!"

For a second the family were frozen, like a trio of perfect marble statues seated around a table. Claire and Eric exchanged another look. Claire whispered to Eric. "Are they broken?"

"I knew it!"

The room exploded into an orchestra of screaming and cheering. Sophia spearheaded the celebration by jumping up from the table and running to meet Claire with a big hug. Veronica and Atticus had risen to their feet too, coming to meet Claire and Eric with a little more restraint. Atticus took Eric's hand and placed a hand on his shoulder, while Veronica pried Sophia off Claire to deliver her own hug.

"Congratulations, son. I'm extremely proud."

"Thanks, Atticus." Eric beamed at his father, looking to the eyes of the man that had carried out this very journey only a few centuries before. Their father/son moment was broken apart by the flying dwarf that was Sophia, who came crashing into Eric, her arms swallowing him whole.

"I knew you could do it, brother! You're not a complete waste of space!"

"Hey, easy now. That's no way to greet the reigning leader of the Belmont family." Eric laughed as he pushed Sophia off him. Veronica simply stood before him nodding.

"Congratulations, Eric. I know we don't always see eye-to-eye on things, but this is the start of a new era within the Belmont family. I will give my life for these kids, you have my word on that."

Eric held Veronica's gaze with respect. "Thank you, sister. That means a lot."

"Now for names..." Veronica began. "I'm thinking 'Veronica.'"

Atticus scoffed. "No, come now. Their grandfather Atticus would be much more suitable surely..."

The bickering was interrupted by the cheering and bawling of Sophia, who was running around the room, punching the air and screaming. "Baby vampire! Baby vampire! When was the last time you saw a baby vampire?!"

Claire and Eric couldn't help but laugh at the mixture of reactions from the family.

"Well actually..."

Claire tried to get the attention of the room, but from Sophia's manic celebration and Atticus's and Veronica's heated discussion of what a suitable name would be, no one was taking any notice. Eric took it upon himself to rein in his wild family.

"Listen up!"

Atticus and Veronica broke their debate and Sophia stopped mid-cheer. "That's not all we have to say. We have more news on top of that."

"Well, well." Veronica raised an eyebrow and folded her arms. "Spit it out then. What could top a baby?"

Eric looked at Claire and nodded. Claire smiled at him, and looked at the family once more, twisting her fingers together in nerves.

"Well that's just it," Claire said timidly. "It's not just one baby. We're having triplets."

Eric and Claire couldn't help but laugh as they watched the reaction unfold all over again, albeit amplified this time. Atticus's pale expression seemed to grow whiter still, and he stood there with his jaw flapping.

"I can't believe it..." His voice trailed off. "This is spectacular news!"

Even the icy-faced Veronica couldn't help but crack a smile. She nodded at Atticus and shook her head in disbelief. "What he said. I can't believe it. Congratulations, love birds. I'm happy for you."

In the background Sophia's voice started up again, louder and more jubilant this time.

"Baby *vampires*! Plural! Can you believe it!"

The group erupted in laughter as Sophia resumed her kinetic celebration. Atticus and Veronica broke into another argument about names. Claire felt Eric's hand tugging at hers. He pulled her to the side of the room, leaving the family to react to the news in their own way.

"I think that went rather well," Eric said. "For my family anyway."

"Agreed." Claire stared up at his pale beauty in adoration, lost in the twinkling red pools of his soul. Their hands twined together and she leaned into him, falling against the solid oak of his torso as he embraced her. His lips grazed her forehead, and she closed her eyes and smiled, smelling his musk as she breathed in.

His hand brushed over her stomach.

"I can't wait to meet them," he said.

"Me neither."

They turned to the window and looked upon the valley below. Their story was just beginning.

ELSEWHERE, LATER.

THE WITCH WALKED THROUGH THE THICK bracken of the jungle, cursing the heat and humidity of the hell she had come to suffer the last few weeks. Her pilgrimage had been a long one, but worthwhile. She delivered the message that no other knew.

Her contact had taken some time to return her message. Once she had her reply she had set off at once, knowing her journey would take a long time. One couldn't simply walk into the council of elders—one needed an invite. Her news was sufficient enough. Her welcome had come quickly as she had expected.

She was at the last of her strength, having used her magic to carry her up the river and across the valley. She had been attacked by something on the border of the ancient ground. Half beast, half demon. She did not know what it was and she did not care; all she knew was that it was some ancient dread conjured up to protect the temple of her clan.

The bush finally receded, and she saw the decrepit shrine of her temple poking up among the dark vines of the twisted jungle floor. Stray shafts of light broke through the thick canopy above. The ever-present cry of the howler monkey wasn't heard here, nor was the constant shrill of the cricket or the heavy wings of the large tropical flies. The clearing stood in perfect silence; even the wind didn't dare to brush through this dark part of the jungle.

She pulled the back of her hand across her forehead, trying to keep the sheets of sweat from dripping over her brow. Her ebony skin shone in the tropical heat. She entered the temple, using the very last of her magic to open her night eyes. The dark recess of the temple shadow grew bright in her vision as if it were under daylight.

She walked the path, taking care not to trip over the broken sandstone slabs, trying her hardest to remember the way. It didn't take long for her to remember. She felt the pull of the grand council guiding her all the while.

Before long she'd navigated the dark maze of corridors that lay hiding under the earth of the jungle. The dark and cramped corridor gave way to a large underground room, which was supported by pillars on all sides. A small opening in the ceiling some distance above granted the only source of light, which drifted down to the floor in a dim shaft.

The pillar of light illuminated three hooded figures, who sat cross-legged in a row on a raised section of the floor. Ezra ascended the steps that led to the podium and knelt before the figures.

"You made it," said the first.

"Yes," Ezra answered. "I've journeyed far, my Queens. I bear important news."

The figure in the center pulled her hood back first, accompanied then by the two on either side of her. Ezra cast her eyes down to the floor in shock, not wanting to waste the ageless beauty of her Elder Queens on her mere immortal eyes.

"You may look upon us, servant. There is no quarrel here."

Ezra obeyed the command of her Queen and looked up with uncertainty. The swirling white eyes of the elder looked back at her, glowing with the ancient earth magic behind them.

The figure on the left spoke, her voice whistling with the same velvet smoke of the first.

"You spoke of great news regarding the Vrakos prophecy?"

"Aye, my lady." Ezra cast her eyes quickly upon the gaze of the second elder, before looking back to the ground out of habit. Each woman was as beautiful, mysterious, and terrifying as the last. "I believe I have witnessed the start of the prophecy. This could be the beginning of the end."

"What are you guardian of? What end do you speak of?"

"Vampire, my lady," Ezra explained, cursing her forgetfulness. "It is the prophecy that foresees the end of man and vampire."

The third elder spoke. "Vampire?"

"Yes. Sorry, my lady." Ezra addressed the other elder quickly. "Vampire. They are what you once knew as Vrakos. Things have changed... the world is different."

"Very well," said the lady in the center. "Tell us of your message. What makes you think the prophecy has come to be?"

"There was a breeder. A human female. A member of the house that I protect, a male vampire—he has reproduced with her."

The central lady on the podium sat forward. Curiosity glimmered over her perfect expression, her face almost glowing in the dark like fire.

"You are certain?" The azure eyes of the elder widened at the implication of the witch's words.

"Yes, my lady. And she has given birth to three vampire children."

All three of the elders sat forward now. They looked between each other and back to Ezra. Ezra kept her eyes on the ground, but she heard the starting of their movement.

"And you are sure this is the sign, Guardian Ezra?"

"It is the first," Ezra answered. "According to the scripture. Three sisters, born in one generation—separated at birth, each human, each breeders to the Vrakos bloodline."

"Very interesting," said the central lady. "Do we know who these other two sisters are?"

"No," Ezra answered honestly. "We have no idea, my lady, but if they fell into the wrong hands..."

"...it could be the end of us all," answered the voices of her elders. Silence beat in the temple for a moment before her leader spoke once more.

"Very well. We must send you back, Ezra. We will return you to the mother earth to do so. You oversaw the first. The prophecy states there is one guardian for three."

"Yes." Ezra nodded quickly, understanding the full implication of the words.

"Remember your mission when you wake, child. Let destiny guide you as she did for the first. You have served us well with your life. Now we must take it."

"Yes, my—"

Ezra's words choked in her throat, as the hand of her leader shot up in the air. The figures remained cross-legged, their perfect faces expressionless.

Ezra lifted into the air, clinging at her throat and kicking her legs into the dark as she felt the life force draining from her body.

A second later she fell to the floor as a corpse. She looked down upon her body through the eyes of her soul. She looked back to the podium and saw the blinding light. The true forms of the elder Queens. Their voices breathed through every atom of the air as they spoke to her one last time.

"Destiny will guide you now. Relax and close your eyes. When you wake you will be in your new body, and your mission will begin again. Find the next daughter and protect her. It is paramount to our very existence..."

She closed her eyes and felt the warmth of the Gaea take her body into the unknown. When she opened them again, there would be white—and life would begin again anew.

By Zara Novak

OTHER BOOKS BY ZARA NOVAK

Tales of Vampires
The Vampire's Slave (Book 1)
The Vampire's Prisoner (Book 2)
The Vampire's Mate (Book 3)
The Vampire's Captive (Coming Soon)

Bad Blood (Coming Soon)

Join my <u>mailing list</u> **to stay up to date. It's for new releases only, no spam:**
http://eepurl.com/b5tmt5

Made in the USA
Coppell, TX
20 February 2024